WAVE OF MUTILATION

Praise for Douglas Lain

"Douglas has a great brain. I am hugely impressed with his prospects to be a completely uncommercial genius. God help him."
—**JONATHAN LETHEM**, author of *Motherless Brooklyn*

"In *Wave of Mutilation*, you will find echoes and shadings of J.G. Ballard, Philip K. Dick, Tim Powers, and Walker Percy (which is stepping in some high cotton). Lain shares an obsessive fascination with the interface between technology and psychology, and has a keen eye for sharp juxtapositions (as in the contrast between eroticism and hygiene). But what I admire especially is his grasp of the subtle and pervasive mood of paranoia and melancholy that haunts our digitalized era—an elusive sense of spiritual desolation complicated by the ghostly infestation of forces and presences we can never really understand. An intellect and a questioner of literary forms, Lain is also a husbanding, fathering advocate for the Everyman in us all. The result is curiously human and intimate—down to earth, even as the universe falls apart in our hands."
—**KRIS SAKNUSSEMM**, author of *Zanesville* and *Enigmatic Pilot*

"It's legitimate SF, and it's 'mainstream,' and it's metafiction: I don't know anyone else doing quite what Lain is doing; fascinating work, moving, strikingly honest, powerful."
—**LOCUS MAGAZINE**

"Doug's stories exist in a space where reality is labile, a space that has its own rules and expectations, and commands a sort of mental poetry."
—**EILEEN GUNN**, author of *Stable Strategies*

"Straight out of the Pamela Zoline era of New Wave fiction, with a strong dose of nuclear paranoia and Reagan-era 'kill a Commie for mommy' reverse-nostalgia, Lain writes from the conscience."
—**JAY LAKE**, author of *Pinion*

"Lain's writing is unsettling, ferociously smart, and extremely addictive."
—**KELLY LINK**, author of *Magic for Beginners*

"The universe has a hole in it and reality is leaking out. Who knew it would be this much fun? Doug Lain's *Wave of Mutilation* is the story of Christian and Samantha; a story that generates itself as it devours itself. Its characters and surreal scenes are rendered with an engaging style and seem to have truths to tell us about relationships, politics, sex, the history of furniture. At the same time, they convince us they are insubstantial, errant, nothing but the illusion of the world. Terrific writing, good laughs, and the flawless execution of a fictional tightrope walk between "reality" and nothing. Wonderfully original!"
—**JEFFREY FORD**, World Fantasy Award winner

"*Wave of Mutilation* is brilliant: a Barthesian examination of structure, a reverse Russian nesting doll of increasing surreality and emotion. To find oneself alternately pondering the metafictional importance of a Sesame Street book and choking back the tears induced by a surprisingly human drama is a testament to Lain's writing. I loved every sentence, every word."
—**J. DAVID OSBORNE**, author of *Low Down Death Right Easy*

"*Wave of Mutilation* is about what everything means. It's what you get when the stuff in your head comes out to play—the love of your life floating in a motel swimming pool, unreality leaking from the world, block parties of identity destruction, and interstitial spaces where you might spot Donald from *Mathmagic Land* motioning you into a strange place between now and a distant childhood that might not even be yours. Lain's writing is sharp and surprising. You'll have a good time."
—**RAY VUKCEVICH**, author of *Meet Me in the Moon Room*

FANTASTIC PLANET PRESS
AN IMPRINT OF ERASERHEAD PRESS
205 NE BRYANT STREET
PORTLAND, OR 97211

WWW.ERASERHEADPRESS.COM

ISBN: 1-936383-96-9

Copyright © 2011 by Douglas Lain

Cover art copyright © 2011 by Paul Groendes

All rights reserved. No part of this book may be reproduced or transmitted in any form or by any means, electronic or mechanical, including photocopying, recording, or by any information storage and retrieval system, without the written consent of the publisher, except where permitted by law.

Printed in the USA.

WAVE OF MUTILATION

Douglas Lain

Fantastic Planet Press
Portland, Oregon

SOLIPSISM BY A MOTEL SWIMMING POOL

I'm carrying Samantha's old portable Realistic brand cassette player, a rectangle of plastic with a red record button on the left side, along with a Styrofoam cup full of lukewarm coffee, and so I have to use my hip to open the gate on a fence with green and white plastic slats threaded between the links. I step gingerly over pebbles and enter the pool area where the smell of chlorine marks this interstice between the hygienic and the erotic. Poolside recliners with blue and white horizontal vinyl straps double-wrapped around aluminum frames serve to neatly barricade off new arrivals from those already bathing, and I stop to consider my next move.

Samantha is already swimming. She and I are either the only guests in the motel or we're the only two compelled to test the claim, permanently posted in neon, that this outdoor pool is heated. From my side of the recliners I ask her about the temperature but she doesn't appear to hear me. Her ears are full of water as she swims on her back, windmilling her arms while kicking her legs.

I place the antique tape player under a recliner, and then

adjust the volume so I can hear the Pixies' "Debaser" over the sound of the highway and Samantha's splashing. I sit down and the vinyl straps on the recliner stretch. It's probably a decade old or older, and the strips are brittle from the years of exposure.

"How's the water?" I ask again.

I'm still dressed in neatly pressed jeans and a rust-colored polo t-shirt while she's naked in the pool. She's skinny dipping even though the pool is surely visible from the rooms on the second and third floors. She gestures at me as she paddles past. Everything is okay, but I'm not quite ready to get wet. I sit on the edge of the aluminum frame, take a sip of my coffee, and shiver even though I don't consciously feel cold.

Something is very wrong with the world is why. A simple pleasure like sharing a splash with my wife or even just enjoying the vision of the pink light from the neon vacancy sign reflected across the surface of the pool and across her skin, these things have to be denied. Instead I focus my attention on the poolside recliner. The recliner has a history. I can think through the iterations of the form of the recliner and this supports me.

A decade earlier, at Denver University, I took a course on modern furniture and it was there that a professor, a man named Krestler, convinced me that even everyday, mass produced furniture has a handmade history. Specifically I know that the swimming pool recliner has an antecedent. Before motels and poolside furniture manufacturers, recliners were built for the officer class in Napoleon the Third's France. Recliner chairs were utilitarian devices constructed out of canvas and steel to serve as beds, chairs, and day beds.

My pregnant wife is swimming underwater. Watching her legs kicking beneath the surface, the slow motion of her round but still intoxicating body, the way her blonde hair undulates across her bare back, I'm tempted. My boxers might be an adequate substitute for bathing trunks. She spins around, slows down and reaches for the concrete wall behind her. Her hair swirls around her face like a cloud of blonde ink and I decide I don't want to swim at all.

Around the same time that inventors were working on recliners, municipal swimming pools were serving a hygienic function in American cities. Manmade chlorinated pools were a remedy for working class filth. The teeming masses would go for a swim in a neighborhood pool and come home a little cleaner. Over time the municipal pool as a public bath gave way to public pools as coed spaces where white bodies were put on display. Segregated swimming pools were erotically charged spaces, and the mode of dress, the "bathing suits," became more and more revealing.

Samantha passes again, still underwater, and my desire for her is replaced by a desire to avoid manipulation. We aren't on vacation. This isn't a holiday.

My coffee is cold now, the vinyl straps I'm sitting on are still descending, and I scoot off of the recliner and onto the damp concrete. Pool water soaks through the seat of my pants, but it's better down here on the hard ground. I get on my hands and knees and reach under the recliner. I want to turn up the music, but reaching under blind I retrieve an old soda can instead. I find a tin can produced by a soda company I've never even heard of; I find a can of Graf's soda. The label is obscured by rust, but I can make out the shape of the logo. There is a curved glass of cola there, and there are suspicious ice cubes inside this cartoon glass.

What I need is a point of reference. I've set up the scene specifically for this. I've got my coffee, an old Pixies album on cassette tape, but my anxiety persists.

The problem isn't just the swimming pool, but the motel. Motels and hotels are like cruise ships or cemeteries. They're spaces that mark a boundary. A hotel is outside everyday life, and when I'd first landed my gig at Holst's Architecture I'd often pursued hotel projects precisely because I'd imagined that these kinds of fantasy spaces would give me more freedom. I thought they'd really let me be creative, but that's not how it was. A motel or a gay spa, anything remotely abject or decadent, these are spaces that frame the television commercial that is America.

A motel has to look like a box, it has to include an orange shag carpet, and it requires the placement of a television set at the foot of the bed. It's a very formal or generic space precisely because it's a transitory, probably extramarital, space.

Samantha is doing laps. She's on top of the water now; I can tell from the sound of her kicking, the sound of her chopping the water. She's doing a front crawl.

An old soda pop can, the smell of chlorine, a chain link fence, and the feel of my wet pants clinging to my ass crack… this is all that's left in the world after the accident? The picture I usually looked at, the image of myself in a world that cohered above the level of rusted soda cans and illicit sex in motel rooms where you paid by the hour, Dad had ruined the image. First his father had worked to blow up this world of appearances and progress with an atom bomb and then Dad himself had let the air out of the world with an atom collider.

How was I supposed to have sex with my wife if the only space left for it was a motel room? Was I expected to make our honeymoon last forever or to pretend that she was my French mistress or an old soda can?

Still, if Dad had accidentally poisoned himself with quarks and neutrinos, if he'd pushed everything into the margins, I'd helped him. Portland key parties, designer hangovers, too many hours spent in motels like this one, all of it had done a number on me too. Sure, good old Dad left me a stupid mess, but I was the one who kept trying to stupidly enjoy it. It was my nightmare too, this life inside the frame.

Samantha isn't swimming anymore.

"Christian?" she asks.

"What is it?"

"Why don't you join me for a swim? The water is warm."

I finally turn to look at her. She's doing the dead man's float in the middle of the pool, keeping her face just above water, and it's a nightmare. In the neon light from the vacancy sign she looks like a censored photo. That is, where her face should be, in the space right at the surface, there is a gap. She's opened herself up again. The mask of her face is split in two. Half of her smile is under her left ear and the other half is under her right. She's opened her face and now pool water is running into her, into the empty spot, the perfect dark oval, where her face ought to be.

"You're taking in water," I tell her. "Like the Titanic."

Samantha makes a gurgling sound like a drain. "It feels good," she says.

FATHER CALLS FROM THE OTHER SIDE OF THE MUSHROOM CLOUD

I expected that the telephone attached to the backlit mushroom cloud at the American Museum of Science and Energy in Oak Ridge, Tennessee would provide an audio commentary for the exhibit, but when I picked up the handset and placed it to my ear, the prerecorded message turned out to be from my recently deceased father. What's more, he seemed to have broken from the script. Rather than relaying the expected sanitized story drawn from the nuclear industry's own institutional memory of the birth of the atom bomb, the voice on the other end of the line addressed me directly.

"I made a mistake, Christian," Dad said.

I'd stopped at the explosion while Samantha was in the bathroom, not because I really wanted to listen to another explanation of the bombings of Hiroshima and Nagasaki, but just because I could stand there and watch the restroom door without appearing as a stalker. So I'd stood there, looking away from the flattened destruction.

Dad's bout with cancer had drawn me back home a half dozen times in 1999 and 2000, but now this time it was over. I was back home in Tennessee, wandering the American Museum of Science and Energy with my absurdly pregnant wife in order to attend his funeral. Dad had been in a lot of pain for a long time, and of course it was wrong to resent him for his timing. Besides, Samantha and I both agreed that we'd take it in turns comforting my mom and watching the news on cable television.

The nation was in limbo. Newscasters and admen stood in front of red maps of the USA, red maps with blue fringes along the coasts, and took turns reporting the impasse. The Presidential candidates made appearances as well, but only in montage sequences. One tossed a football to his daughter on the lawn of the vice presidential mansion while the other chewed his lip and stared blankly out of his hotel window. James Baker and William Daley did all the talking while the candidates sat on their hands.

"Is anybody there?" Dad asked. "Christian? Can you hear me?"

What was really disconcerting was how Dad kept addressing me by name. Maybe he was talking about Christians, using my name as an adjective? Maybe Dad was just describing the character of the Manhattan project.

"Christian?"

I didn't answer him because it was impossible that I was hearing him at all. Also the phone wasn't really a phone, but just a mechanism for listening. It would be silly to talk into it.

"There was an accident in the lab. The accelerator amplified the gap and we didn't expect that," Dad said. Or I think that's what he said. I was only half listening. I held the phone up to my ear, kept my back to the mushroom cloud, and stared blankly at the display labeled "atomic pioneers" on the other side of the exhibition room. I followed the orange carpet with my eyes, a tracking shot, and settled on the cardboard cutouts of Oppenheimer, Einstein, and President Truman. The dead president had been photographed in a skimmer hat made of straw and decorated with a red white and blue hatband.

These were the great minds of the Greatest Generation. They'd devised a way to realize man's dream. They'd finally delivered the power we really needed. Gas chambers and punch cards were inefficient, and the great men ran equations and fit together the pieces for something better. After they finished, the next holocaust would be a push button affair.

"We altered the TV's gravity and accidentally hit static," Dad said.

Samantha was taking forever. I tried to imagine what she might be doing in there. I thought of her bulbous belly under her thin sundress. She'd taken to locking her fingers together under her round belly in order to support the weight of her own girth. She had to carry her belly with both hands when she walked.

I wasn't ready to be a father, wasn't interested in funerals, and as far as I was concerned the zero years had arrived too soon. I'd spent my twenties convinced that I'd been born at the end of history, and this was good news as it meant that my status as the low achiever in the family no longer mattered. I might have spent my childhood washing down Ritalin pills with swigs of Jolt cola, but the end of history meant that my embarrassing degree from a second tier State University, and my having settled for a career in an entropic city like Portland, none of that mattered. If the 90s were on the other side of the end of history then I was off the hook, and a year earlier, back in 1999, I hadn't worried. Instead I played around with different architectural styles. I hadn't even tried for a promotion, but just drew connecting lines on graph paper and tried out triangles. But once I was in the year 2000, I wanted nothing more than to erase those lines. What I guess I wanted was to build a pure blue space.

"During the accident in the lab the accelerator amplified the gap. We didn't expect that."

Samantha finally emerged from the restroom, but she didn't join me by the mushroom cloud. She turned toward the oversized glass model of the hydrogen atom instead, and stopped there. She didn't look at the model; she wasn't longing for a chance to see past electrons and into the nucleus, but was looking underneath. She opened her hands below her round belly and leaned over to talk to a couple of young boys who were playing around the base of the structure. One of them, a dark haired kid in leather sandals and a lime green iZod shirt, scooted around so it appeared he was holding the giant atom on his shoulders. He was a preppy boy version of Atlas under a glass world and I imagined that if he shrugged he would send the atom rolling into the glass panes of the other exhibits. The boy might end up smashing the replica of the Enola Gay that looked so shiny and right in its protective glass case.

"Pay attention," Dad said.

It was very strange to hear Dad's voice on the phone. I didn't like it very much really, so I hung up. I didn't need any trouble, especially not from my dead father. If I had to take a phone call from a dead relative I'd have preferred to talk to Grandfather. He had lived through a depression and a World War and might still have something important to say. Dad had grown up on Howdy Doody and McDonald's. His was the first generation of permanent childhood. What did he know?

My mother smiled at me. She stood by the silver sphere on the Van de Graff generator. The generator produced blue sparks and Mom smiled, reached out, and then put her hand down on the ball. Her long grey hair stood up straight, wildly flowing toward the ceiling.

And then the phone hanging next to the mushroom cloud let out a trill. It was ringing.

My father told me how a man could go on living even after he died. Apparently, even though the soul doesn't exist as something separate from the body, ghosts are real. A dead man can pass through walls and/or occupy a telephone attached to an exhibit at the American Museum of Science and Energy. A ghost can say boo or move random objects, like a kitchen chair or a mop say, across a room. A ghost can make you hallucinate monsters or trap you in a television set. All of this can go on, but only if the ghost fails to realize that he or she is dead.

"Think about those Road Runner cartoons where the Coyote runs off the side of a cliff and then remains suspended in midair. He'll only fall if he looks down," Dad said. And this was the secret. Life itself was a matter of refusing to look down or, if one couldn't avoid looking, then the trick was to find a way to look without seeing. People could withstand almost anything if they followed that simple instruction.

What had happened is that the particle accelerator in Oak Ridge, the one Dad was working on when he was exposed to the radiation that gave him cancer, had poked a hole in reality and, apparently, unreality was leaking out. Not reality, but unreality was leaking out. The experiment had gone very wrong and our solar system had been flattened into nothing. Still, as long as nobody looked down, the idea of life could be maintained for a little while longer.

"What I need is that you help me maintain the idea that I've got going," Dad said. "This accident might even be a good thing. Sometimes death is the best cure."

Even though Father was dead, his body burned into a pile of ashes, and even though he seemed to know he was dead, he seemed more confident than ever.

"You have to do something for me, Christian," he said.

"What is it?"

But he couldn't tell me. He said that what I needed to accomplish couldn't be captured with a direct, positive description. Instead of telling me what to do, he just described all the ways I'd already gone wrong. He stacked up examples for me as I listened through the phone attached to a mushroom cloud.

For example, in 1987 I'd failed to have sex for the first time. That is, I was a virgin at the time and I tried to have sex with a girl, but I didn't manage it.

I'd never told anyone about it, certainly not my dad, but being dead he was privy to a lot of confidential information. Dad reminded me of this girl who was not a cheerleader in order to help me understand what he wanted from me.

Gia hadn't passed the audition for the cheerleading team but she had been willing to take off her yellow sweater for me. We were dating and I think finally offering herself to me had been some sort of compensatory act after her disappointment in the gymnasium. During her audition she'd climbed to the top of a pyramid of other girls in yellow sweaters and blue polyester skorts and then panicked. Gia had lost her purchase on the shoulder blade and hipbone of the girl beneath her and, after the fall, she'd ended up in the boys' locker room with me; she'd ended up handing me her bra.

First we'd found a way to stay in the school overnight. We'd hidden under the bleachers while the audition for cheerleaders continued, waited under there, our bodies pressed up against each other in the stale darkness, and then when the doors closed and the silence had lasted for what seemed to be long enough, we'd ventured out.

"Why aren't you hard?" she'd asked me after she removed her yellow sweater and her socks. I remembered her standing naked under a stream of hot water. We'd hit the showers together. Gia had a nice body, plump in places, especially around the hips, but overall just what I'd wanted. Her pubic hair had been a bit lighter than the frizzy brunette curls on her head, her breasts were a bit lopsided, but I had wanted her.

"You want to do it?" I'd asked. And she'd said yes.

But it had been impossible. Even if I could have gotten hard enough we hadn't been able to find a comfortable place to lie down. For example, the wooden bench in the locker room was too narrow, and standing up in the shower was too unstable. I kept slipping. We'd tried it on a desk in a geometry classroom and then on a couch in the teacher's lounge, but I'd been too frightened or something. Exposed and inadequate, I couldn't maintain my desire and penetrate.

I was on the phone with my dead father and he told me the whole story. He reminded me.

"This cheerleader is still your primary sexual fantasy ten years later. She broke it off with you and you never did fuck her. You had to settle for her best friend, that red-headed girl named Maggie. You two did it in the backseat of her parents' Ford station wagon?" Dad asked.

"Yeah."

"But never with Gia. And now she's what you think of when you're having trouble. The memory of her in the shower always does the trick."

I didn't like Dad talking about her. It was obscene. He sounded like describing Gia worked for him too. That was nauseating.

"Don't worry," Dad said. "I won't ruin her for you."

The particle accelerator hadn't torn a hole in reality but in our collective fantasy. The problem wasn't that reality was disintegrating, but that unreality, fantasy, was slowly seeping out of the world. My father's machine had punctured the world and it was my job to patch the hole.

"Think of the universe as a birthday balloon," Dad said.

"The balloon is leaking?"

"No," Dad said. "It's more like we've partially erased the words 'Happy Birthday' that were printed in red ink on the side. That's the problem. It's the message that is fading."

EGGS AT THE AIRPORT

I was standing in front of a row of leather and steel seats at the Knoxville International airport, staring at a television screen mounted to a horizontal beam just below the off-white ceiling panel, and considering what syndrome Samantha would connect to my symptoms if I confessed that I'd experienced a haunting. If she said that I was experiencing something like schizophrenia that would only make things worse. Schizophrenia was precisely what my father's ghost had predicted. He'd punctured the universe, illusion was seeping out, and all that was left in the world were all the stupid contingencies. But, if she said I was hallucinating due to lack of sleep or that I was hearing Dad's voice because I was grieving, that might be worse because it would mean that what I was feeling was somehow normal. I didn't really know what I wanted to hear.

There was a pane of glass between us and the runway to our left, and the sterile concourse labeled B to our right. CNN's John King smiled down from the screen, his teeth glowing through pixels as he waited silently for his cue.

"Oh. Yes," the anchorman said. "These are headlines."

The Republicans in the Miami-Dade court system were

paranoid about the machines that would be used to sort out questionable ballots and they'd informed a Miami judge that these machines would inevitably damage ballots that contained votes for Bush. The sorting machines apparently had a built-in bias for democrats.

"Miami-Dade will begin a manual recount of votes despite Republican objections," King said.

The anchorman's awkward smile, the way he would pause and raise his manicured left hand to his chin, this was how a television personality maintained the illusion of continuity. The story he was telling was one of systemic failure but what was communicated through these routine gestures was the exact opposite. Yes, ballot boxes had gone missing, chads were clinging to ballots, and the count was disrupted. It still couldn't be a real disruption, but had to be a harmony. The country was a perfect balance of red and blue.

Maybe it would be enough just to tell Samantha what had happened and know that she knew. I would still be haunted but I wouldn't be alone with the knowledge. I might not understand any better, but I would at least know that we were both confused. I would have at least that much.

George Bush's attorneys asked the Florida Supreme Court to instruct the State to decide the outcome. According to the Republicans, Congress should've just picked the winner. Meanwhile, Miami-Dade County began a manual recount.

Was this a prerecorded message, or was it live? Was the admission of the contingency, this confession that the election would be decided by a fight in the courts rather than by the will of the people, a way to inoculate the viewers at home, to build up an immunity to future irregularities and contingencies, or was this a real accident that couldn't be covered up?

Standing in the terminal, in front of the leather seats, looking at the perpendicular lines of shiny armrests and the clean orange carpet beneath my feet, I felt as though I was maybe in some sort of sacred space. I was watching a news program from another world, but as long as I was breathing cool stale air I would be okay. The airport, the mounted monitor, the way sunlight filled the room, all of it gave the impression that I was outside of history and could enjoy the view.

"I want to tell you something," I said.

Samantha nodded. "Okay. But I don't think it will help you much."

"What's that?"

"I'm pretty sure I don't exist," she said.

I looked away from the anchorman on the screen, away from the televised teeth, and examined my wife.

"Is that like a Zen riddle or something?" I asked.

Samantha shrugged and took another sip of soda, and I looked her up and down. People said that pregnant women had a tendency to glow, and that was certainly true in Samantha's case. She was glowing in her jeans with an elastic waist band sewn in. She was glowing behind the yellow blouse that fit her like a funnel. Narrow at the top and wide around her belly. I thought of how she'd come by her condition, of my responsibility, and reached out to touch her belly.

"You exist," I said.

"I'm pretty sure I don't," she said. "I'm a bit frightened, actually."

I told her that I was looking right at her, and then I reached out and put my hand on her belly. I was touching her. She was carrying our child.

"I don't think I'm really pregnant," she said. "Or if I am pregnant then whatever is inside doesn't have anything to do with me. It's hard for me to explain."

I started to say something to that, but she stopped me by holding up her index finger and then pointed to her mouth. I just had to wait, she indicated, and then she'd explain it. But when Samantha opened her mouth no sounds came out, and instead of teeth or a tongue her mouth was filled with the round white surface of an egg. She put her hand to her mouth and removed it for me. She handed me the first one, the first egg.

"Bravo," I said. That was probably a mistake because she put her hand over her mouth again and then produced another egg for me right away. This one was blue like a robin's egg, only just a bit larger. She was pulling chicken eggs, or maybe duck eggs, out of her mouth. The next one was green with speckles and the next light brown.

"Okay. Okay," I said. "Something's gone wrong. I understand that. My father already told me that something has gone wrong, but could you please just hold it in for now? We've got to catch this plane."

Samantha handed me another egg. And when we did board the plane I couldn't sit down right away but had to stand in the aisle while Samantha gagged and handed me another half dozen. I figured we'd never get off the ground because of them. We were in coach and Samantha was in the aisle seat coughing them up while I stowed them in the overhead bin. I lined them up along the seam in the back, along the line where the bottom of the bin met with the wall of the plane. I almost dropped a few eggs, but managed to wedge them all in. I had to reach over a briefcase and a folded over garment bag in order to find a space for them.

An older lady wearing a grey polyester pantsuit hobbled down the narrow aisle and bumped me with her walker, right on the back of my knee, sent me sprawling across Samantha's belly.

"Pardon me," she said. But she spoke flatly and then stopped there at our row.

"Excuse me," I said right back. I grabbed onto the armrest and worked myself back into the aisle. Samantha turned to the lady, opened her mouth, perhaps to speak, but instead produced another green chicken egg. She spit it into her palm and held it up for the lady.

"I'll take that," I said. I took the egg from Samantha and then stopped to examine my wife's reflection in the window on the right side of the plane. I could see the lights from the airport, the red and green dots along the runway, on the other side of my wife's transparent profile. Samantha was a spectral presence on the surface of the window and to see the world outside I had to look through her. And when she opened her mouth to produce another egg, I put my hand over her mouth.

I put my hand over Samantha's mouth and told her to

swallow. "We've got a dozen up there in the luggage rack already. That's enough."

She closed her eyes and her throat moved as the egg slid back down her throat. She grabbed my arm and looked me in the eyes, and swallowed hard. Her fingernails pinched my skin even through my sports coat.

"Swallowed?" I asked.

Samantha made a retching noise, a noise that reminded me of all that can go wrong inside the human intestinal tract, and then let out a long belch.

Sitting down for takeoff, listening to the eggs roll back and forth in the overhead compartment, watching the yellow lines on the runway and then seeing the ground fall away, I was sure my dead father was watching. He was just outside the window, out on the wing standing where the sunlight reflected along the silver edge, or if I turned around and looked back toward the orange and red curtains he was back there and just out of view.

When we reached a cruising altitude, the flight attendant brought us plastic cups with ice and cans of Coca-Cola and placed these on the tray tables that folded down from the seatbacks in front of us. I stirred my beverage but held off tasting it. The thin stream of cool air from the valve overhead felt good on my scalp, and I was afraid that if I took a sip the sweetness, the feeling of bubbles passing over my tongue, would be too much.

Samantha grabbed my hand, stopped me from stirring my Coca-Cola, and placed my hand over her mouth again. I felt the smooth surface of eggshell between her lips and then, when she swallowed the egg, I felt her tongue and her warm spit on my palm.

GOOGIE ARCHITECTURE

After watching her swim in the pool I left Samantha in our room and then returned to our car, to the parking lot, just to get away. I'm out here trying not to think. I don't want to go back to the room, not right away, so I'm considering the motel, thinking about architecture.

I'll start with the Palm Tree that marks the spot where the drive meets the street, then turn and look at how the motel floors stack on each other like layers in a sheet cake. Whatever functionalist aesthetic an unadorned rectangle might normally convey is undone by the spectrum of colors on the outer walls. There is a kernel of early 20th century modernism here, sure, but by the time this place was built modernism itself had been overcome by technicolor. This motel is a rainbow sherbet structure, an exemplar of space age wonder. The style is called Googie and Googie was an architecture born into the service of roadside commerce. Cars and suburbia meant that commerce would colonize spaces beyond America's urban centers and Googie was what this colonization looked like. The original McDonald's golden arches were pure Googie.

She's waiting for me probably, but I pace back and forth in front of the rectangle and try to decide whether or not it's worth defending. Yes, it is tacky. It's ugly and ridiculous, but at the same time you can't say it's mute. It means something. It reminds passersby of Tang and moon boots. An optimistic building, this sheet cake says that human beings have a destiny. It promises a b-movie future rather than more dreary survival in an airless, technocratic, everyday life. This motel almost takes our old ambition for self-transcendence seriously, but not quite.

I wonder if Samantha has managed to drain away the chlorinated water she took in during her swim. I walk up the drive and touch the rhizomatic trunk of the palm tree. The fronds are rough to the touch and seem to stick out crazily.

The trouble with motels and bowling alleys, with the Space Needle and golden arches, is that these structures are knowing. These are kitschy spaces that insist that you enjoy imagining what it might be like to visit Mars or have sex in zero gravity.

No, I can't side with this motel because it's really too much. It's perverted. The motel is a fantasy that can never be realized and somehow the motel itself knows this. The motel wants you to lie down on a vibrating bed and watch yourself jiggle in a full-length mirror while fantasizing about the Apollo missions and all the lonely wives our brave astronauts left behind on Earth.

In the lobby I'm secretly thrilled by the track lighting, the orange carpet, the retro cigarette and Coke machine, and I purchase a pack of Lucky Strikes and a bottle of Coca-Cola. Then I lean against the check-in counter. I lean across and am disappointed to discover credit card scanners and laptops stashed away behind the 50s facade.

This motel was perverted from the start. The architect worked in a populist mode. He aimed his work at an ignorant mass audience who by definition believed in Googie's space age future, but there was never a point in Googie when it believed in itself. Kitsch is thought of as naive, but nothing can be kitsch until cynicism is introduced. That is, it's only when somebody can laugh or mock a place like this, only when somebody like me comes along to buy Lucky Strikes and Coke ironically, that kitsch is born.

Samantha says she isn't real. She's shown me. She sank to the bottom of the swimming pool and then waited for me to join her there. After I pulled her to the surface, over the concrete edge, while I watched the water drain from her left ear, she just blinked and tried out reactions. Her facial expressions didn't really settle down into anything fixed, but she just kept flipping through them. First she tried a smile, then a smirk, then a frown, and then an open-mouthed look of shock.

I sit in the lobby for another few minutes and enjoy the sound coming from the color television. For me this is as close to any kind of meditative silence as I can stand. I'm next to the no smoking sign by the front door and I'm watching Al Gore take questions from a pack of exasperated reporters.

How much longer will he soldier on in the face of voter impatience? Doesn't he think it's time to let the country off the hook?

"I think I probably don't exist," Samantha told me.

Was she like the motel, a fantasy that could only persist by declaring its unreality, or was she what she appeared to be? And if she was a projection, just my fantasy, then why was she telling me? Did I really want to know? Was I trying to communicate with myself through her? And if that was right, if I was trying to tell myself something, then why did I need to use her, need to fantasize, in order to communicate? Why couldn't I just be me without her? If she was my fantasy then what was I?

"I'm convinced that I've won," Gore said. "And it's my duty to press on until every vote is counted."

I take a sip of Coke and then step out of the lobby and into the night air.

In the parking lot, by the palm tree, I light a Lucky Strike cigarette even though I usually don't smoke and take another swig from the green glass bottle. If Googie architecture is kitsch, what is a wife who demands you recognize that she isn't real? Have I gone completely insane?

I take a long drag on my cigarette and think it over.

A BLOCK PARTY IN FLUX

There was always a sense of urban community inscribed into the craftsman style bungalows that lined our block, a certain utopian communalism put there by William Morris, but when our taxi turned onto Hawthorne and I stared out the passenger side window, past the perspiration on the glass, to find our neighborhood transformed from a sleepy cul-de-sac into something like a pagan festival, I was surprised. There were at least a dozen barbecue grills on the sidewalks and smoke flowed into the half circle of asphalt and obscured my view of handcrafted yellow porches and oak doors with inset stained glass windows. The toppled lawn chairs and recliners with aluminum frames and multi-colored webbing were splayed across organic gardens and concrete drives like crime victims.

It was a block party, but there were far too many neighbors involved, considering it was a November weeknight, and far too much exposed flesh out on the street.

The cab driver seemed stunned by the sight of it too. Instead of asking for the fare, this Algerian man lit a clove cigarette and just watched. We sat there in his idle cab—he'd even turned off the meter—and watched a college girl named Lucy strip out of her red denim shorts and her off-white sleeveless button-up blouse. She stood there in her panties while her landlord, a retired lawyer who'd let his grey beard grow long and who looked a little like Walt Whitman but more like Charles Manson, took much longer to get out of his tweed jacket than she'd taken to strip completely.

There were teenage boys standing on the picnic table behind them, and the one in a baseball cap and jeans that hung down low on his ass worked to open a beer bottle with a lighter while his friend was stripped out of his Dockers and argyle sweater.

"That'll be forty-two dollars and eleven cents," the cab driver said.

What at first looked like an orgy was something more complicated, something stranger, than that. These neighbors weren't fucking or even groping each other, but were just exchanging clothing. And some were just observing. The fat man who'd moved to our block from Bend, the one who used too many chemicals on his lawn so that it always smelled toxic, stared at his neighbor's shriveled genitalia as the younger man handed over a sweat-stained muscle shirt, a pair of blue Nike sweat pants, and yellowed briefs to an old lady named Susan. Susan smiled and reached inside her purple blouse, up a billowy sleeve, in order to unhook and remove her bra.

Somebody had set a portable CD system, a grey boom box with tinny speakers, up under the picnic table. I'd never heard the song before, and the lyrics were indecipherable. There was just a stubborn beat and an occasional word like "swimming" and "mind."

"Let's go home?" I asked.

Samantha nodded and reached out for my hand. I was already carrying a black Samsonite suitcase, a heavy and cumbersome thing, but she put her small hand over mine and held my ring finger. She pinched me, caught the loose skin between my wedding ring and the hard plastic handle of the suitcase. I put down the luggage in our yard, on the soft green lawn, and popped my finger in my mouth.

"Welcome back to the lawless land of Portland," one of our neighbors said. I didn't even look in his direction at first, but it turned out it was Kevin. He was the husband of Samantha's friend Michelle who in turn had known Samantha's sister Becca when Becca had attended Denver University when all of us had been young.

Kevin was wearing his wife's blue jean mini-skirt and a lime green halter top that I had never seen on Michelle but which didn't look like it belonged to Kevin either.

"Lawless?" Samantha asked.

"That's right," Kevin said. "Want a beer?"

"We just got back," I said.

"Oh, come on now. Exchange your clothes and then join me for a beer."

I took a moment to glance back down the street, at the houses across from ours and then at the red and brown bungalows on our side of the street. Our neighbors had opened their curtains and turned their television sets toward the windows so the CNN logo was perpetually in the periphery.

"Change clothes with Samantha and we'll play ping-pong. I pulled the table out of the garage. See? Over there by the dumpster? Also, I've got a little weed."

The next song from under the picnic table was Herman's Hermits' "I'm into Something Good." The college girl from the duplex was wearing her landlord's tweed coat with nothing underneath and had her long blonde hair hidden under his fedora. She was taking sips from a tall boy can of Coors while her roommate put on a pair of purple polyester pants that belonged to her landlord's wife.

"Whose idea was this?"

"Whose idea?" Kevin asked. "Whose idea was this?"

"Yeah."

Kevin laughed and punched me lightly in the stomach, just hard enough to get me to bend and react, but not hard enough to knock the air out of me. "Come on. Change clothes with Samantha, or with Roger over there, and then we can get stoned."

I picked up the Samsonite suitcase and duffel bag and shook my head. It was all too crazy for me, I didn't swing like that, and besides I'd just gotten back from my father's funeral.

"Your dad?" Kevin asked.

"That's right."

I took a step toward our front door, toward the wooden goose and rainbow windsock on our porch, but stopped again when I heard the click. Kevin had something, some handheld device that he was using to make a clicking sound at me. He made just one clicking noise with it, one very audible click.

"Stop there, pal."

"What's that, Kevin?"

"It's a .32 I think. I bought it last winter in case the whole Y2K thing turned out to be a real problem."

I told him that I'd purchased some bottled water and a couple dozen cans of Spam under the same pretext, but that I wasn't about to fetch the Spam and make him eat it right there on the front lawn.

"Exchange clothes with Samantha."

"What is this about, Kevin?"

"Now. On the lawn, and while there's still light."

Samantha's maternity underwear fit but the elastic in the waist of her pants had stretched out so I had to hold them up with my hand while I fished her 36D cup over my right arm. I tried to catch her eye but Samantha was focused on buttoning my khaki pants. She might also have been holding back from vomiting up another egg. The trousers just wouldn't fit around her hips, and so she pulled my boxer shorts up over her belly and folded my khakis over the iron rail that divided our front steps.

"You look beautiful," Kevin said. He looked me up and down. I was wearing Samantha's white button-up shirt but it didn't fit around the shoulders so I left it unbuttoned. I also left her bra loose around my chest. The panties were nice and snug though.

Kevin wanted to talk politics while we played ping-pong. He wanted to get stoned, enjoy the cool night air out in the cul-de-sac, and talk about the popular vote, the absentee ballots from the soldiers stationed overseas, and how it all came down to the perception that Gore had lost.

"We're going to end up with Bush," Kevin said.

"What's that?"

Another couple had paired off to change clothing in the street. The middle aged couple who lived around the corner, her name was Maxine and at forty she was fit while her husband was not. Watching them I couldn't focus on the game. Her g-string looked uncomfortable and obscene on the fat lawyer's ass, while his tighty-whities kept slipping down on her, exposing the top of her neatly trimmed bush. When she tried to tie his paisley tie, a novelty gift with huge red paisleys on a field of yellow, her husband's underwear fell to her knees.

Kevin kept serving one ping-pong ball after another and I just let them bounce away. I stood there sipping a Coors and took it in. Not everyone was a transvestite, but nobody was who he or she normally was. Everything was switched around, and somebody rolled out barrels of ice cream. Tubs of Rocky Road and Sherbet were set down in the middle of the street and grownups in footie pajamas, college girls in sweat-stained Hawaiian shirts, and accountants in wonder-bras lined up with cupped hands.

"Christian, your serve."

The half-decade since I'd moved to Portland had been measured in block parties just like this one. Fourth of July fireworks, New Year's vomit, Halloween candy hoarded in secret, stolen from children, all of this was normal. Even the ping-pong game at gun point, the forced transvestitism, fit the pattern. Many of the guests I might expect to see weren't present because this event was spontaneous and local, but otherwise it was part and parcel of the expected. And if anything truly disturbed me as I set up my serve, as I swung my paddle down and sent the hollow orange ball sailing just above the net, it was the easiness of it. Wearing panties that squeezed my balls, feeling Samantha's bra slip off my shoulder, it was a humiliation I already knew. I was comfortable with it.

"Nice one," Kevin said. He picked up the orange ping-pong ball and tossed it back to me. "Can you do it again?"

I didn't want to. I wanted to go home, to trek my bags to the front hall where our plush off-white wall-to-wall carpeting and mahogany hat stand with an inset mirror would be waiting. I put down my paddle, set the paddle on the dividing line, and held up my hands. I showed Kevin my palms.

"Don't shoot me?"

"Whatever."

I found Samantha sitting on the front steps of our house next to a pile of eggs. She'd pulled the luggage up to the steps, put the Samsonite in front of her as a kind of a barricade, and was drinking lemonade from a tinfoil bag. She was no longer wearing my clothes but had changed into blue silk pajamas and a green knit cap.

"How do I look?" I asked.

Samantha put her elbows behind her, leaned back on the porch, and closed her eyes as she spoke. "Nobody believes that they believe they believe they are free," she said. Then she looked up at me expectantly as if I knew what she was talking about, but I had no idea. I just wanted to get away from the party, maybe watch the election coverage, and stop thinking or trying to think. Beliefs about beliefs gave me a headache and what I wanted was another drink. Maybe I could get a scotch and soda from Frannie or her husband. I thought I'd seen them. She was wearing a beige suit two sizes too big for her and a fat red tie while he was in lipstick and heels. They always brought Scotch, good Scotch. I'd ask them for lemon.

"Something is happening," Samantha said. "Everything is in flux. Everything is equal, but if you ask people what they think or how they feel they say they're just as stuck as they were before."

I sat down next to her and asked her how she felt but she said she was fine. That she was better. There were fewer eggs now, and she was feeling more substantial. I picked up one of them, a blue egg that was a bit smaller than was typical, and held it out at arm's length between my thumb and index finger. I examined the egg under the porch light.

"It's not the election," I said. "Something went wrong with the super-colliders. Reality has lost its mooring. Dad said that unreality was seeping out or getting erased. Everything is in flux."

Samantha asked when my father had mentioned this to me and I told her that he'd spoken to me before his funeral but after his death; I explained that he'd spoken to me through an exhibit at the American Museum of Science and Energy and she put her palm on her forehead and bit her lip. She pointed to a man whose hairy ass was hanging down below the hemline of his girlfriend's miniskirt. The man had left the skirt unzipped and unbuttoned and it just barely fit around his waist. He looked squeezed, uncomfortable.

"Do you think he feels the flux? Is he labile or part of a flow?" Samantha asked.

"Of course not," I said.

While I'd been playing ping-pong she'd asked people why. In between speaking eggs and storing them in her left pajama pocket she'd asked Kevin's wife Martha. Martha whose working class background was evident even though she dressed fashionably in Pendleton sweaters and sheer skirts. The body she put into her trendy clothes was tubby, from years spent eating Doritos on an old orange couch with holes in the upholstery. Martha had smiled and nodded when Samantha asked what was motivating everyone to switch around.

"It's terrible, isn't it? I know," she said. It wasn't something important to her, it wasn't even a game she particularly enjoyed, but in order not to disappoint the neighbors, in order to go along with everyone else, she'd switched clothes with Kevin, and she was helping to organize a looting expedition.

When Samantha told Martha that the game seemed important to her husband Kevin, that he'd held the two of us at gunpoint and insisted, Martha just laughed again. It was all very funny.

Another egg, a plain white egg like the kind you'd find in a supermarket, came out of her mouth and I took it from her and then picked up the Samsonite suitcase.

Outside, the neighbors gathered in the middle of the street to discuss their plan. They were armed with hoes, sledgehammers, and brooms, but watching them I wasn't worried. I closed the venetian blinds, took the white egg to the kitchen, and put it in the fridge, in the crisper. I pushed a gallon of milk to the left and found lemon juice in a green glass bottle, tracked down some honey in the cabinet, and then mixed and heated honey and lemon juice together in a small sauce pan. I found a coffee cup, the one with a brown, red, orange, and yellow rainbow and I took the hot lemon and honey to Samantha in the bedroom only to discover that she'd solved her egg problem in the meantime.

What had happened was that she'd found a lever on her right side. It looked something like the kind of plastic operating lever you find on spring-loaded toasters. It was right below her ribcage, above the hip, and when she'd pushed it down her stomach opened, her belly flipped out like it was on a hinge. She was sitting on the bed, with her belly open, taking out the eggs.

I handed her the teacup and she held up her index finger as if she had an idea.

"Watch this," she said. Inside of Samantha there was a wooden shelf, probably pine, and it was held in place by two small bones connected to the outer wall of her body. On the shelf, next to the few remaining eggs, there was a paper cup, a wax Dixie cup, filled with a warm yellow fluid. Samantha drank down the lemon juice I'd given her, then reached inside herself and removed the Dixie cup, and handed it over to me. I took a sip.

"Lemon juice and honey," I said.

"Am I dying?" Samantha asked.

I just stared at her, at the flecks of white paint on the wooden shelf in her belly, at the flesh-colored shell of her body, and wondered what it meant or how it was done. I pulled the blankets off her and pushed down on the mattress. But the mattress was soft and yielding. There was nothing suspicious about it.

"And what about the baby?" Samantha asked. She looked very concerned sitting there, until she removed a table lamp from the stand next to our queen-sized bed and placed it on the shelf. The table lamp was a bit too tall, the bulb was in her chest, but Samantha closed her belly, pushed until she heard the click of the latch, and then gave me a smile.

Light came out of her mouth. Somehow the lamp had turned on inside her, and she took on a pinkish glow.

It was at that moment, when her mouth became a spotlight, that I remembered what would happen next. That is, I remembered that Samantha had always been hollow. In the very first scene at the motel swimming pool Samantha had been swimming without a face, and she'd let herself sink, let herself fill up with chlorinated water in the motel in Oak Ridge. I also remembered that the motel in Oak Ridge was in the present tense. Googie architecture, a heated pool, the history of the poolside recliner, that is all happening now, while the bedroom, the pile of discarded chicken eggs, the Dixie cup filled with lemon juice and honey, all of that was in the past.

"We're trapped," Samantha said. "More stuck than ever."

I wasn't sure just exactly when she was speaking from. Was she telling me something that would be in the past from the perspective of the now that was a motel room in Oak Ridge, a now that should be considered the future when considered from the past that included her discovering a lever?

"It's okay," I said, although I wasn't sure who I was trying to convince. Was I telling the me who was thinking back on the story from a motel lobby, the me who would be stuck in the parking lot of the architectural firm where I worked, the me who would be frightened in the wooden tunnels the housewives and their impotent husbands would build over Hawthorne Boulevard? I thought I was probably there, speaking from a fortified interstitial space, somewhere dark that smelled of ceiling insulation and sawdust, but what I saw was that I was still sitting on the bed with Samantha. She was opening her head for me, swinging her smile open wide so that her eyes moved off the surface of her face. Her face broke into two pieces, one half pushed out and then slid back until half her nose and her left eye were below her ear.

"I'm not going to lose the baby," she said. Her voice was coming from an abyss at the center.

I was going to answer her, to ask her to clarify, but I was interrupted. After Samantha opened her head, the neighbors arrived.

It was Kevin who put his foot through our bedroom window first, and then he stepped aside as a man behind him swung a sledgehammer down hard and cracked our windowsill. Then a third man, a dentist named David whose last name I could never remember, put his fuzzy slipper-clad foot through the open space Kevin had made, and I jumped out of bed and grabbed him. I grabbed David's leg and shouted obscenities through the gap in our wall, but David and his wife—I can't remember her name—pushed back and I found myself sprawled on our oriental throw rug at the foot of the bed. Our neighbors clambered in with us, David and then Kevin, in an unashamed and even somewhat mechanical manner. Looking out the gash in our wall I saw that they weren't the only ones waiting to get in. There were maybe a dozen more: men and women wearing bathrobes, t-shirts, fuzzy slippers, bowties. They milled about in the yard like extras in a George Romero movie.

"Get out, Christian," David told me.

"What's that?"

"We're going to flatten your house. We're going to tear down the walls."

THERE IS A MONSTER AT THE END OF THIS BOOK?

When Samantha was eleven years old she visited Europe for the first time and it was there, on a Swedish playground, while playing on a jungle gym painted orange and black, that she first realized, and then rejected, the reality that was her own strangeness. While climbing on a concrete play structure in Stockholm, an undulating biomorphic sculpture that was matronly and curved in such a way as to encourage a child's touch, she was approached by a native. A Swedish boy, a boy who was perhaps a year or two younger than she, tapped her on the shoulder and he, naturally and without any pause, spoke to her in his native tongue. She was mystified, of course, but she did manage to communicate her lack of comprehension by confidently speaking to him in English as if he ought to know her words. After a time, they came to the only sort of understanding that an eleven-year-old American girl in blue jeans and Keds sneakers and an eight-year-old Swede wearing proper leather shoes and shorts with suspenders might plausibly come to. They climbed on the play structure, the castle thing that seemed to have emerged from a grey lava lamp, and as they played their conversation grew louder and louder. They climbed, laughed, skidded back down, and all the while understood that nothing like communication was possible.

Samantha likes to think that they became friends.

"Still, I took it for granted that it was he, and not I, who was alien," Samantha told me. "I was a stranger maybe, but what was really happening was that I was in a strange land." The realization of her strangeness in this other boy's eyes did not convince her that she was odd, and instead of wondering if what she took to be solid and real was just a seeming, if what she took to be necessary might be contingent, she looked to her parents and felt confirmed in her position as their daughter. She somehow managed to perceive the scene from some imaginary cloud, or as if it was all happening on television, and she smiled at how indecipherable and strange the Swedish boy, with his ruddy cheeks and woolen pants, had turned out to be. Sweden was a funny place. It was no wonder that God didn't usually watch this channel.

Samantha spent many hours reading books that she'd brought with her on the plane. For instance, she recalled reading *The Secret Garden* and *The Mouse and the Motorcycle* during that trip. However, she never mentioned a book that she was far too old for, but that seems to be an important book given her situation, our situation. It's a picture book put out by Golden Books and the Letters PB and S back in 1971. What Samantha probably didn't read that summer was the classic: *There is a Monster at the End of this Book*. But this book starring lovable old Grover holds the key to understanding what went wrong on that playground in Sweden, what went wrong at the neighborhood block party, and why I had hung up the phone on my dead father.

In *The Monster at the End of this Book*, Grover reads the title page, is frightened by the promised monstrous ending, and sets about trying to stop the story he's trapped in from being read. Grover becomes terrified as the pages turn, but I think the drawings of him stacking cartoon bricks in order to stop the reader from turning pages, somehow connect with the Swedish boy and that concrete, egg-shaped play structure, because what Grover proved was that breaking the fourth wall just propels the plot. That is, even though Grover can see that he's in a text, even though he knows that he is being read into existence by a stranger who he can't see, and even though he knows that his future is set in advance, he nonetheless struggles as if he believes he is free. Even as he admits his fictional status, Grover becomes more and more afraid, more and more convinced of his own existence, and more committed to the initial premise in the title.

The ending, the moment when Grover realizes that he himself is the Monster mentioned, is deflationary. What had scared the little muppet no longer frightens because he assumes that being Grover is the most normal thing in the world.

Grover says, "Well, look at that! This is the end of the book and the only one here is…ME. I, lovable, furry old Grover, am the Monster at the end of this book." Grover should be overwhelmed by his own fictional status. He should be devastated to realize his own monstrous strangeness, but instead he remains lovable and furry.

A NEIGHBORHOOD BUILT ON DESTROYED ARCHITECTURE

Our cul-de-sac had been razed to its foundation. The roar of demolition and riot had, over the course of hours, slowly given way to an awful quiet as we realized what we'd done to ourselves, at which point I'd crawled into bed next to Samantha and we'd both looked up at the stars. She'd lain there next to me, not talking but just opening and closing her mouth so that the light from the lamp in her belly seemed to blink on and off. She might've been signaling people on Alpha Centauri or Sirius, but it didn't matter.

The next morning I tried to hide under our comforter. I pulled the overstuffed blanket up, ducked my head under, and felt a breeze on my feet because I'd pulled the comforter too far.

A few of the two story houses still had staircases but they didn't lead anywhere. Pipes and beams stood exposed to the morning light because our homes were gone, and broken plaster and glass littered the ground where there had been wall-to-wall carpeting, hardwood floors, or linoleum tiles, but most of our furniture remained: our queen-sized bed and nightstand, the bathtub and toilet, a loveseat and the glass cabinet for the entertainment center, and so on.

I gave up on hiding, sat up in bed, and stared through absent walls at the college girls in the duplex across from us. They were in the ruin that had been their bathroom and the redhead who I sometimes saw sitting on their front porch, she'd been smoking long cigarettes after a night out when I'd stepped out to fetch the morning paper, was on the toilet while the more friendly girl with short black hair stripped out of her orange silk pajamas, stretched, and adjusted the knobs in the porcelain bathtub. The brunette put her hand under the showerhead as if to test the temperature of a stream that was never coming, and then pulled back the shower curtain. Plaster billowed across the room and dusted the redhead's straining face as the smiling girl stepped into the tub and closed the curtain behind her.

In the house next to ours, Martha and Kevin were arguing in the space that had been their kitchen. They were standing next to an electric oven that periodically shot sparks over their heads. The partial frame behind their appliances contained dangling wires and broken pipes, and on the second floor, in what had probably been a guest room, there was a continuous bubbling flow of water and a snaking live wire. Steam, sparks and water fell into the space that had been their living room, a steady trickle to the spot where their leather sofa absorbed the black water.

Samantha got out of bed and approached the space where there had been a door to the bathroom. She mimed the process of turning a knob before stepping across the imaginary boundary and then, once she was behind the invisible door, she stood in the mud and looked at the mirror that was hanging from a nail in an intact structural beam, hanging above a geyser that marked the spot where our sink had been. Samantha looked at herself and put her index finger up against her chin. With her other hand she unbuttoned her pajama top and it fell away from her torso and into the mud.

Samantha leaned over and pulled down her pajama bottoms and then stood naked in the space that had been our bathroom. She looked at her left profile and then the right side and her index finger remained on her chin. She moved while the center stayed the same. She made ridiculous faces, pressed her nose up and snorted like a pig, and then she grabbed hold of her left shoulder and pressed down. After a moment of strain her left arm popped out slightly from her shoulder. There was a space between where her arm usually attached and the arm itself, but something inside the arm, wires or plastic cartilage, held the arm in place. Then she used her right hand to trace out an indentation near the base of her neck and when she pressed down there a horizontal split appeared in her neck. Her head was still attached to her spine, but there was a gap.

Stop. I wanted her to stop, but Samantha removed her blonde hair from her perfectly smooth scalp. She'd been wearing a wig all along and I hadn't known, and when she dropped this wig into the mud I shouted involuntarily.

Samantha proceeded past this. She put both of her hands to her head, covering her ears, turned her head left and then quickly right so that her head detatched. The lightbulb from the table lamp was just peeking up out of her decapitated body. Light that had been contained in her skull reflected off the mirror, and turned away. I put my feet down on the cold and muddy floor.

I got to the front lawn by following the pattern of everyday life. I opened doors that weren't there, turned down halls that could no longer be said to exist, and then looked out at the lawn through a window in empty space. The automatic sprinklers were on. I stepped out the front door, was careful to go around a wayward stream from the bent sprinkler head, and then found the wall.

There was a wall in the street. My neighbors had built it. They'd walled off the street with the thin wooden boards that had been under plaster or brick the day before. The boards were nailed to vertical beams, one on top of the other lengthwise, and I walked the curve of the cul-de-sac and found that there were two walls. The street was covered. The housewives and their transvestite husbands had fortified the road with pieces of what had been their homes.

The walls were partial, there were plenty of gaps, but I recognized it as the wooden tunnel that I'd remembered the night before. This was the structure that connected the fragments of my life together. What had been impossible and out of sequence before might make sense if I followed the path that had been sealed off for me. I had no neighborhood, no wife, nothing, but I could at least find the door in on this structure. In fact I remembered just where it was. And when I found the entrance to the long shed, to the crazy tunnel, it was unlocked just as I knew it would be.

Unreality, the disappearance of a center, meant that I had a destiny. My dead father, my disappeared wife, the destructive neighbors, all of it made sense. All of it meant that an ending had been arranged in advance and that God was looking out for me.

I stepped into the tunnel, between the walls, held out my arms, examined the pattern of light and shadow on my forearms and palms, and headed north.

AN INTERSTITIAL SPACE

I was inside something that was more shell than structure. The boards, the stripes of light that passed through the gaps, gave the impression that I was somewhere that I ought not to be. This was the underside of reality, the secret core of the world, and as I walked through it I remembered that I'd been warned. My father had warned me that unreality was leaking out of the world, and he'd said that what we needed was a new fantasy. Without it, without some sense of wonder, some detail that could fill in all the gaps and make us believe, all that would remain would be this kind of flat reality.

I walked on cool asphalt and tried to remember what would happen next. Then I opened my cell phone before it could ring and listened for my father.

In the semi-darkness, in the narrow corridor that was nothing but the demarcation of a limit, the voice on the other end of the line wasn't my father at all, but was the voice of a narrator. He was calm, assured, and from another era…probably the fifties or sixties. This was a voice from nature documentaries or educational films made by Disney, and he wasn't addressing me directly but was speaking to Donald Duck.

"The mind knows no limits when used properly," the voice said. "Think of a pentagram, Donald. Now put another inside, a third, and a fourth. No pencil is sharp enough to draw as fine as you can think, and no paper large enough to hold your imagination. In fact, it is only in the mind that we can conceive infinity."

The movie playing through my cell phone was *Donald Duck in Mathmagic Land*. Specifically I was at the end of the film, at the scene where Donald created a hallway lined with doors. That was the infinite space of Donald's imagination. The doorways were simple rectangles, golden lines drawn on a black background and positioned to create the illusion of three-dimensionality. These rectangles were each one smaller than the next as the pattern approached the center of the screen, or as they appeared to be further back or closer to the vanishing point.

It was a familiar space, a space that could only exist on film or in a cartoon. In the cartoon Scooby Doo, for instance, Shaggy and Scooby would frequently encounter this hall, and it was always the site of a sight gag. They'd run from one door to another pursued by funhouse monsters. Frankenstein or Dracula would open one door, one on the left side of the screen maybe, and Scooby and Shaggy would magically come out of the door on the right side.

This hall, this nowhere space of the mind, was the space I was travelling through. Only, my hallway had no doors. In a real world like the one I was stuck in, in a world without fantasies, the doors disappear because the miracle of dislocation that usually operates off-screen can no longer be relied upon to work properly.

Unreality was leaking out of the world because Dad's particle accelerator had popped a hole in the story.

WORKING THROUGH A CONCRETE BLOCK

The parking lot on the other end of the tunnel was, in one sense, empty. There were no vehicles between the white rectangles on the asphalt outside of Montgomery Park, but when I stepped out between these lines and shielded my eyes from the daylight I found office workers sitting where their BMWs or broken down Toyotas should have been. White-collar types were resting on spinning chairs and leather couches: Architects, stockbrokers, attorneys, real estate agents, and okay, two hot dog vendors from the food court (teenage boys in chef hats and orange aprons). They were staring out at the horizon, at the place where the blue sky met the commercial landscape, but this horizon was broken. It no longer appeared as a straight line but veered off at a right angle. The horizon cut right and off the page, and everyone smiled at the sight of this line set askew.

I approached them, started with my immediate supervisor whose name was Jason and who was two or three years my junior.

"I'm sorry I'm late," I said. "What's going on?"

Jason acted as if he didn't hear me at first and then, when

he was finished examining his fingers and palm, he slowly spun his chair in my direction.

"Christian Nicholson," he said. "You decided to show up today."

Jason looked relatively normal, didn't appear to be wearing women's clothing or makeup, but it was impossible to know what might be under his Dockers pants.

"Why are we in the parking lot?"

"You're lucky, Christian. There has been some sort of accident and nobody has been able to get inside today. Management in New York is even considering sending everyone home early."

"I can go home?"

"Not yet. New York is still deciding," he said.

"But we can't get inside the building?"

"No."

It turned out that Montgomery Park was full of cement. Somehow the facility, every inch of it, had been filled with quick-drying cement. In order to create a cast of the structure, in order to reproduce the interior space, quick-drying cement had been chosen. It was a simple process that was relatively cheap. The whole project ran under budget in fact, and now all that was left to do, according to Jason, was to strip the outer walls away.

"We did this?" I asked.

"It may have been a project that our firm was involved in, but please do not go around repeating that," Jason said. "It would be embarrassing and might even open us to lawsuits if any of our colleagues in the building were to misconstrue the facts."

"You mean it would be a problem if the lawyers on the second floor got wind of what we'd done."

"We didn't do anything. I, myself, may have made a few calls and sent a few memos, but those were on the level of an inquiry. We were gathering information. There was no official policy and I have no knowledge of any policy of implementation. We ran a feasibility study."

"A feasibility study about filling the building with quick-drying cement?"

"That's not accurate. We were originally considering plaster."

The man lying on the desk next to Jason's swivel chair, the man whose blue oxford cloth shirt was unbuttoned so that his hairy chest was exposed to the sun, interrupted his sunbathing on office furniture and spoke. He shifted on the steel surface of his desk, turned on his side, and then moved his mirrored sunglasses down so he could catch my eye.

"I think I was the one who did the research on materials. I priced the cement," he said.

"You did?"

"I believe so," he said. "It's really weird, isn't it? And now we can't get in the building."

And it was at this point that I remembered my own role in the project. Before flying to Oak Ridge, I'd place an order for 143,000 square feet of quick-drying cement. I'd ordered 4,500 tons of the stuff. I'd even started planning how we might begin the process of filling Montgomery Park. The best way would be to pump it in from the bottom floor. The fluid would work its way up without putting too much pressure on the top floors or breaking furniture.

"Since we knew about this in advance, why is the central office stumped about what to do?" I asked.

"We didn't know about it in advance," Jason said. "That is, we do not know for a fact that we knew about this in advance, and you should not say that we do or did."

When I considered the project as an architect, thinking of the solid block of concrete inside Montgomery Park as a design choice, I wasn't sure how to label what we'd done. I stood at the entrance and looked at the wall of grey we'd made, and considered how the mall was now useless. We'd replaced the interior space with something solid.

Was this a postmodern gesture or a Brutalist intervention?

Brutalist architects wanted to reveal the structure underneath the usual facades in order to compel people to recognize their own complicity in the structure's presence. Most people resented buildings that made this sort of demand. Paradoxically, the exposure of complicity is almost always perceived as an imposition. On the other hand, postmodern architecture artfully recreates the trivial and contingent in order to expose how there are no structures. Strangely, these buildings sometimes include facsimiles of structural elements. A postmodern approach might use devastated spaces, exploded traditions, exposed water pipes that run along vertical seams, in order to give the impression all that is left in the world are remainders or ruins of previous ideologies and epochs.

What we'd done was fill Montgomery Park with concrete, and this was not only an impediment to work, it was also the cause of our understanding what we'd done. I'd been part of a collective effort to organize an event that would lead us to understand how each one of us had been part of such an effort.

I caught sight of myself in the glass door. Looking at my reflection in the glass it seemed that somehow I was standing in the space between the doors and the cement inside, and I wondered if maybe what was true of the cement block was equally true of everything else that had happened. Were my own fingerprints to be found on the collapse and destitution of this story I was telling myself? I didn't remember choosing any of it, but then again no choice or decision can ever really be free.

The architect Louis Kahn's brutalism was a forced choice given that the International style, the unadorned fact of modernism, was dominant when he arrived. The dominance of modernism meant that Kahn's spiritual impulses had to work through the imperative to create unadorned cement buildings without ornamentation or 'style.' What this meant was that Kahn's monuments to eternity and God were grey and rough.

And even Kahn's religious impulses, his aim to transform the modernist aesthetic into an approach towards the monolithic or monumental, was a forced choice. His need to build spaces that spoke to something that transcended mere physical function was said to have sprung from an accident. Kahn's face was burned by hot coals when he was a child and this accidental disfigurement pushed him to construct permanent and transcendent structures. The knowledge of his own frail impermanence pushed him to the realization of a brutal transcendence.

Every character in every story is both limited by the structure of the language employed to tell the story and is the very fiction that transforms the language into the story. Without the fiction of a character or a story, without the emptiness that is at the center of all the accidents, all the burning coals or imposed styles, without an architect, there really would be nothing at all…nothing but dumb reality.

Christian would never be going back to work in Montgomery Park again, but he could still be an architect. The trick, Christian realized, was to assume the empty space where accidents happen as his true self. And then, by disappearing, he might get a grip on the story he was caught in. He might even write a few lines of it. Looking at his own reflection and then past it, Christian realized how he was the architect of his own evaporation, but before he could finish the thought he st—

BREAKING THE FOURTH WALL

Breaking the fourth wall had the peculiar effect of creating a feeling of déjà-vu. Knowing that the world around him was somehow less than it appeared to be, that his story was being told and had no substantiality in itself, created the impression that he'd lived through the moment before. His life was blocked out in advance and it was as if he was performing on a stage or appearing in a television program taped in front of a live studio audience. During his trek back to the Hawthorne neighborhood, Christian walked outside the wooden walls on 1st Avenue and Lincoln. He counted his footsteps as he followed the curb, then he turned and crossed the sidewalk.

His feet clad in Armani loafers sank into the lawn in front of what had been an orange and tan bungalow but what was now just an impression left in mud.

Breaking the fourth wall meant that Christian could move as the crow would fly. He could get back to Samantha and that strand of the plot by following a straight line. He didn't need to find an interstitial space but could just pass through neighbors' yards and houses, like a ghost walking through walls. He was just an idea in a fantasy and this meant that the rules no longer applied.

Apart from the strange determined freedom he found himself enacting, his invisibility was the next big surprise. He was being read, the world itself was a kind of act, and knowing this gave him the power to stand outside the text. He was able to get enough distance from the lawns, boxes, housewives, broken sprinklers, and junk mail brochures (envelopes marked with gold foil or displaying color reproductions of red and white logos and gear), so as to be able to realize that he was nothing other than the words junk, mail, broken, concrete, housewife, or bored.

In one of the devastated houses on the west side of SE Hawthorne, a handsome housewife in a short rust-colored polyester skirt decorated with sunflowers was lying on her back in the mud. She was staring up at what she thought was an optical illusion. The pattern in the textured plaster of the low ceiling appeared to be moving, but was, in fact, not there at all. She was staring up at a clear blue sky.

Christian stood next to her, in what had been her living room, and watched as she moved her bare legs idly and reached out to pluck an alphabet block from where it had gotten wedged between a floorboard and a broken cinderblock. This young wife was vacant, or she was dreaming of something, but she paid no attention to the eight-month-old in footie pajamas who crawled a semi-circle around her head and dragged the letter U with her. The eight-month-old stopped, stuck the cube in her mouth, and tasted mud.

"Are you all right?" Christian asked.

"He always tells me it's just simple," she said.

"Who?"

"My lover," she said.

"Your lover?"

"Well, he's my husband now, but when he watches television he seems like maybe he's my lover again. I like to watch him all glazed over like that," she said.

"Where is he now?"

"Maybe I'll make him a frozen pizza and let him watch cable television. He won't complain if there isn't dinner if I don't require conversation," she said.

"Is he at work?"

"This is the letter A," she said. And Christian realized that she hadn't heard him at all. The conversation was a happenstance or coincidence but not communication. She might hear him, but not directly. To her he was just a shift in the pattern on the ceiling, or the vague memory of a television program she'd seen back when she was just a little girl in 1989.

"Not a television program," she said. "A pop song. You're going to drive your car into the ocean."

By the time he arrived back at the frame around what had been the foundation of his house, Christian knew the title of the book he was stuck in, but not before passing through brightly colored walls, some lime green, some lemon yellow. Going back, he climbed up and down stairs that were no longer real and trespassed through houses that were no longer standing.

However, when he reached his own frame, he used the front door.

"What are you looking at?" he asked the shell that had been his wife. He found her sitting in a wicker-backed chair in what had been their kitchen and staring down at a curved outline, the outline of her own body. There was a print in the dust and dirt on the few tiles that remained. She was sitting on an island of checkered linoleum in the midst of soft black mud.

"I built something," she said. She glanced up at her husband, but wasn't sure there was anyone looking back at her.

He stared at her from the perspective of the mark that she'd left on the linoleum.

"I'm going back to see my mother," he told her. "Back to Oak Ridge."

"You think she can help you? You think my mother-in-law might make this better somehow?"

They weren't going back to see Christian's mother at all. They were going back to Oak Ridge in order to build something, and in order to see Christian's dead father. Samantha understood what her husband needed to do, and how she might help him. She looked at the empty outline of her own body on the linoleum tiles and realized it.

Something shifted. Samantha didn't know what it was exactly, but she knew that much. Something had happened so that the story didn't belong to her husband anymore.

SEX IN A BED

She doesn't have any internal organs; she can open up her chest and pat the wooden shelf inside. Anxiety is a constant. She'll accidentally catch sight of her hand, her arms swinging as she walks across the orange carpet (from the queen-sized bed to the motel bath) and she'll try to breathe, to catch hold of her body. She can feel herself breathing, but knows it can't be a real feeling. She knows that she ought to be dead.

Samantha is rifling through her Samsonite suitcase for a specific pair of grey fleece sweatpants, a pair that she'd made into cutoff shorts a decade earlier. She'd been wearing them when she first met Christian. They were flimsy shorts and when they'd ended up together after the dorm party he'd struggled to untie the drawstring while she'd slipped her hand down his jeans. He hadn't been able to untie the string and finally just pushed a pant leg aside.

The shorts are objectively ugly, but she pulls them on over her bathing suit and sits where she'd placed the white motel towel on the edge of the large bed.

Holding onto an idea of her identity, even though the idea is a fiction, is what she's aiming at. There is nothing at the center, she's seen how there is nothing, but maybe she can accept the nothing. She's empty, but the idea of the baby inside her is real. What is real are her memories of being somebody's little girl and growing up in Manitou Springs. She remembers listening to Brian Eno and getting stoned with her friend Cynthia from the high school debate team. They explored the rock formations in the Garden of the Gods, and she'd worried she might get crushed if the formation called Balanced Rock finally toppled.

Water from Samantha's swimming suit soaks through the seat of her grey fleece shorts and into the towel. She tips her head to the right and a stream of chlorinated water pours out of her left ear. There is a puddle on the pleated coverlet and Samantha breaks from her pose and goes back to the bathroom in order to drain her head. She stands in the tub, places the top of her head against the white tile and turns until she can enjoy the feeling of water pouring out of her ear. She feels the water splashing against her bare legs. It is while she is in the bathtub, while she is focused on the way her cold wet skin makes her feel plausible, that she hears the door to the motel room creak open.

She hears the sound of a television commercial, something about the power of toothpaste and germs.

When the water stops draining out of her she steps out of the tub and catches sight of her reflection. There is a crack down the center of her face. The two sides of her smile are unhinged but she doesn't want to open her skull again. She's not willing to step into that void again just to make a cosmetic change. Instead she runs her fingers along the thin black line between her eyes, watches her own hands in the mirror, and then turns away from herself.

Samantha walks to a spot in front of the television. She blocks the picture of ballot counters in Florida, men and women sitting around a metal table and examining ballots with a magnifying glass and using tweezers to sift through each one, and lifts her left pant leg so as to show him the strip of black Lycra underneath. She lifts her pant leg for him and then reaches back blindly and turns off the election coverage.

"This is impossible," Christian says.

Samantha approaches Christian. He's sitting on the towel she'd set on the corner of the bed. She sits in his lap, puts her arms around his shoulder.

"If I'm not here then how did you pull me out of the pool?"

"I don't know," Christian says.

Samantha scoots out of his lap and then reaches out for the spot where she'd been sitting. She unzips his pants even though she's sure that sex is impossible. Somehow that fact just makes it easier for her to take hold.

"It seems like you have two choices if you want to fuck," Samantha said. "If I'm not here even though I'm sitting right next to you on this bed, if I'm just a projection or something, that would make sex masturbation. You're really doing this to yourself. Or, you can try to believe that I am here. I'm real just like you are. If that were true then sex would be a way to work out your pleasure on my body."

"More masturbation," Christian says.

"It's a dilemma."

The bed is still damp under the towel they're sitting on, and the orange, red, purple and blue patchwork patterned coverlet is tucked in tight between the mattresses. Four flat pillows, two stacks of them, are under the coverlet up by the headboard. And the frame of the bed is poorly designed. The top mattress tends to shift as nothing is really holding it in place.

On the other hand, Samantha is glad to discover, the sheets are clean.

THE GREAT SAND DUNES

She'd suffered sunburn, her shoulders dark red, her legs and arms the same color, as a consequence of their falling for each other. It had been nearly a decade and they'd come up with multiple and various stories explaining the courtship, but this was a detail that they both agreed on. There were other details, they'd taken a physics class together and had paired off to experiment with Slinkies, and they'd both tried their hand at video editing for the University's closed circuit television station (they'd spent a few nights working on cuts and setting down voiceovers), she'd even convinced him to undergo an experimental trial she was assisting her psychology mentor perform at Steinbecker labs, but none of these events or moments were original. All of the other stories they told one another about their past, about how they'd come to be entwined, were variations or repetitions on this one when she'd let her shoulders get sunburned.

She'd been dating Christian's roommate and he'd suggested that the three of them take a road trip to the Colorado Sand Dunes during spring break. Samantha had just started out with Paul, they'd only slept together a few times, and she'd been a bit put off by his insistence to bring along a third wheel. She thought he was wanting to show off for his roommate. He'd needed a witness to their romance maybe, or even more crassly, he'd wanted Christian to overhear them making it. Paul drove a yellow 1989 Jeep Wrangler and the smell of gasoline and vinyl nauseated her as she imagined how audible Paul's grunting would be through the orange polyester fly on their tent.

"It's all very rugged," Christian said as they were jostled left and right in the open jeep.

"What's that?" she'd asked.

"I'm sorry. It just seems odd to me. We're headed for this inhospitable landscape, these shifting sand piles, and we're doing this intentionally. What are we hoping to find there?"

She'd been wearing a green one-piece bathing suit, khaki shorts, and pink flip-flops and when she turned to look back at him, the smell of gasoline fumes and sweet suntan lotion in her nose, something shifted in Samantha and she involuntarily rolled her shoulder forward. She flipped a strand of hair behind her ear and smiled.

What they found when they reached the dunes was that the terrain was more than just stupid sand. They stopped to remove their shoes. Christian and Paul had to roll up the legs of their blue jeans in order to wade across the small stream that defined the boundary between solid ground and moving hills and when they reached sand Samantha stopped, turned to face the two men, and showed them the palm of her hand. She indicated that they should pause.

"Music," she said. And Samantha produced a Realistic brand portable tape recorder from her backpack. She pressed play and the soundtrack from Lawrence of Arabia could be heard at the base of the first dune. Traversing the first hill, over the granular flux, they were carried forward by her soundtrack and a sense of something happening. It wasn't that listening to "Video Killed the Radio Star" and then the Cantina music from Star Wars was in itself significant, just that as they climbed a peculiar nostalgia for the present moment, a recognition of their responsibility as the originators of the moment, took hold. The music worked against the landscape, so that rather than being overwhelmed by the senseless beauty, instead of retreating into their own thoughts as a defense against the fact of the seeming dumb immortality of the rolling hills, they played at having an adventure.

"Are we looking for the Ark of the Covenant, or the Pacific?" she asked.

Paul had a brochure from the giftshop back at the Great Sand Dunes Oasis campground, and he explained how the dunes were twelve thousand years old, that the sand was from the Rio Grande, and that the wind lost power as it crossed the Sangre de Cristo Range.

"Feel that?" Paul asked. He put his hand on her hip, hooked his thumb in one of her belt loops.

"Your hand?"

"The sand. It's still coming. The dunes are always growing," Paul said.

Christian didn't talk about geology, but looked out at the impossible landscape and seemed to take it in. They were at the apex of the first dune and he stopped there while Paul let gravity pull him forward and down.

"When I was a kid my parents took me to a pizza parlor in Washington State," he said.

"You going to tell me a story?" she asked.

"It was the kind of place where the waiters and waitresses wore styrofoam skimmer hats and red and white striped shirts, a facsimile of a twenties or thirties style pizzeria," he said. "There was a player piano and a closed off balcony where mannequins wearing bow ties and oversized sunhats, Victorian ladies and gentlemen, were seated at tables decorated with dried flowers. The mannequins were set in pairs, facing each other, and as the player piano pelted out the "Maple Leaf Rag" or some other Scott Joplin masterwork, I wondered how a future restaurant might set up the same scene, only with people from the present, kids wearing Star Wars t-shirts and adults wearing wide ties and low cut but billowy blouses. If they were to commemorate the present in the future, they'd need at least two balconies. They'd need mannequins dressed like television era Americans, but they'd also need the flappers and sophisticates from the twenties.

"In the future, nostalgia would need three floors," Christian said.

"What do you mean?" she asked.

He wasn't sure, but the mannequins seemed to have come from an era when life was consciously staged by the people living it. "Back then history was happening."

Standing at the top of the first dune, looking down on her ex-boyfriend, feeling the sun on her back, squinting against the sand in the wind, Samantha listened to the next song on her mixed tape. "Beach Blanket Bingo" was a good joke for the moment she was in, and they both laughed at it.

Looking back on it there were other moments that might have more concretely marked the beginning of their relationship. The first time they made love, for instance, had been months later, after she'd ended her relationship with Paul and after they'd attended a screening of the movie Ghost starring Demi Moore and Patrick Swayze, but it was that nonsequitur and her response to it that was the original moment.

"Back then history was happening," he'd said.

And she'd replied with a question, with a hope. "Maybe we can start it up again?"

SHELTERING THE FAMILY HOME

It isn't so much that Christian's mother Nancy is okay with her son's idea to build around her house but rather she appears to be too stunned to object or even comprehend. The rented crane is lifting the aluminum and plastic frame up over her yard and the men in orange hardhats and blue jeans leave footprints and cigarette butts in their wake as they set the first piece into the metal groove.

"You two are going to live with me?" Nancy asks.

Samantha just shrugs. They're going to live in the yard, inside a new frame that Christian is building around Nancy's house. She'd explain it, but Samantha is pretty confident that this information won't clarify anything for her mother-in-law. Since she'd lost her husband Nancy had seemed to be getting better, a bit more confident and less put upon, but now she's out on her lawn, standing next to the curving asphalt that connected all the 50s and 60s bungalows and ranch houses into something that nobody could quite mistake for a neighborhood, and seeming crushed by the bizarre demands coming from her son.

"Christian," she says. "Is this because of the radiation?"

Christian doesn't answer his mother but leaves her waiting

as he talks to a worker in the cab of a flatbed truck. The man looks a bit like Burt Reynolds insomuch as he has a mustache and enjoys chewing gum.

The idea behind the project being perpetrated on Nancy's daisy and tomato garden is this: By encapsulating his family home in an industrial shed he will protect ideas from reality. The world's collapse, the gender bender, the presidential drama on television, all the different ways everything had flattened out like so many empty adjectives printed on paper, was the result of the collapse of the fourth wall. The problem was the lifting of the invisible barrier between the story and the reader.

"I have to create a fictional space," Christian says.

"Can you do that? I mean if this is just a story then anything you do in it will just be another part of it, it will follow from what came before," his mother tells him. "Your father died and then he haunted us both. He told us that the world was going to become real. He warned me to get all of my money out of the stock market," she said.

"He talked to you?" Christian asked.

"I was his wife, of course he talked to me," Nancy says.

Christian spits out the wad of gum that the man in the flatbed truck had given him. He goes to his mother and grabs her by her shoulders.

"Mother, what did he tell you? You've got to tell me everything he said."

Nancy breaks free of her son's grasp and then starts walking to the south side of the house. She seems to be following the footprints in her garden. She stops to fret over crushed basil plants, reaches out and tries to correct the situation, to correct what has been broken. She stands the basil plant upright, but it just collapses again.

Christian follows her. "Mother, tell me."

She stands up and looks at Christian with anger in her eyes.

"What did he say? He asked me to tell him what to do," Nancy says.

"And what did you tell him?"

"How would I know what to do?" she asks.

Samantha tries to explain the new space that her husband is aiming at to Nancy. She tells her that it will be an aluminum framed dream. It isn't that the industrial shed will protect the house from the environment or radiation, but rather that Christian wants to irradiate the space inside the shed in a new way. The industrial shed is a perfect, rectangular breadbox, and Nancy's home is soon to be trapped inside.

"In between the door to the shed and your front door there will be an open space."

Nancy points at Samantha as if she has thought of something, an objection that will stop them and save her yard. A sheet of aluminum hangs over their heads; it slowly swings over the roof of Nancy's green bungalow, just missing the chimney, and then is lowered slowly down to a point where four men in orange hardhats are waiting. The men balance the rear of the shed so that it stands vertically, as another set of three men haul the steel foundation, a slotted beam, to the spot.

"There is a contradiction at work here," Samantha says, but Nancy is walking away from her. Her mother-in-law is shouting at the men to stop but she can't be heard over the repetitive beeping of the crane, or over the sound of metal sliding against metal.

There is a contradiction at work in the architecture just like there is a contradiction between Samantha and Nancy, or between Samantha and Christian, or between Samantha and her own hollowed-out interior. Every part of the building Christian planned is constructed from industrial, synthetic metal or plastic. It will be nothing but a shell put around another form, but even though the stuff of the plan is meaningless and inert, even though there is nothing dignified about the structure materially, the way the pieces fit together generates meaning of its own.

"Think of how a museum has its own feeling. Each room in the Met or PAM has its own shape, its own feeling, even though it is just where one displays art." She stops in the mud that was Nancy's back lawn and puts three fingers in her mouth. Maybe this building is a mistake.

Are they putting her mother-in-law's house in a museum? Are they creating a new living space or are they continuing the deflation, the catastrophe, the crisis?

Nancy is bumming a cigarette from the worker with a Burt Reynolds mustache.

She coughs and then approaches Samantha.

"Where did he go?"

"Who?"

"Your husband and my son, the great architect, where is he?"

Samantha looks back toward the house and then shrugs.

"He's in his room. That's where he is. He's hiding in his old bedroom. He figures all this will go on without him," Nancy says.

And that's where Samantha finds him. He's sitting next to a sewing machine, in between a few cardboard boxes that have been stacked on the single bed that used to be his. There's a poster left over from his teenage years above his bed: an illustration of a pale brunette whose nude hourglass figure is an absence in a black triangle.

Samantha holds up her hands in front of her face and touches her thumbs together in order to make a space, a square in the air. She looks at her husband through this frame and then turns in a tracking shot. She takes in the scene and finds the center, the point that all the action is revolving around.

On the television screen on top of Christian's dresser there are blocks of light: green, yellow, and brown blocks. The light creates a scene with a forest in the background. There are rolling logs and a pixilated little man running right and left. A white scorpion is crawling through a dark space on the bottom of the screen.

"You're playing a video game?"

Christian doesn't answer but on the screen his little man descends a ladder into darkness. The figure runs and then jumps when it reaches the white scorpion, but Christian's timing is off and there's a synthesized wah-wah sound as the hero blinks out of the game.

Christian starts over at the crocodile pit. A vine made of blocks of light swings toward him.

"Was there ever a real space?" Christian asks.

"How do you mean?"

He points to the screen, to the upper half of the screen where there are trees and then to the dark half where cartoon icons of scorpions lurk.

"I thought I had depth, that there was my surface self and then my own real self inside, but look at this game. The surface and the underworld, day and night, both are on the same flat screen."

Samantha sits down on one of the cardboard boxes on his floor, and then stands up again. She considers the bent flaps and how they are tucked together in order to seal the box. She wonders what is inside. What is solid enough in that flimsy box to have supported her weight?

A NEW SPACE?

On December 13th, Al Gore conceded the 2000 presidential election and Samantha stained the orange carpet in the industrial shed. Her water broke.

The next day, at 3am, she gave birth to a seven pound three ounce baby girl in Penrose Hospital. The little girl's Apgar scores were seven and nine, and she was born with a full head of thick brown hair.

Now it's January 20th and George W. Bush is on the television. The screen shows the new president with his hand on a Bible; he's repeating the words Supreme Court Justice Rehnquist gives him. The old judge looks gloriously authoritarian in his robes. He's wearing the same robes he wore when he presided over the previous president's impeachment proceedings, the robes with gold stripes on the sleeves.

There are thousands of protestors lining the presidential parade route. There are men and women in down jackets, parkas, knit caps, and green mittens. They hold signs that read "Depose King George" and "Hail to the Thief!" They are surrounded by men in black helmets and black jackets holding batons.

The furniture in the shed is color-coordinated and stylish.

The aluminum roll-up walls are the same autumnal orange as the carpet, and the sofa and loveseat are the color of red delicious apples.

Christian's mother is in her house and sitting at the second floor window, looking from her bedroom. She's watching the big screen television from up there, looking down at a spot in what had been her front lawn.

The mob of anti-Bush activists are herded back, out of the picture or outside the frame, and the president promises to uphold the US Constitution, in sickness and in health, or until the commercial break.

The space Christian and Samantha created is open and clean. There are plenty of standing lamps inside the shed, but not too many. There is enough light but no glare, and they have plenty of privacy too. There are curtains that close for privacy. In this good light, in this neutral space, Samantha's face is seamless.

Looking in on it all through a hole in the aluminum wall, seeing this through an absence, you consider whether this constitutes a happy ending. You realize that this story is very nearly finished now and pause at the end of this sentence in order to consider other, more satisfying, conclusions.

The space you can see through, this hole in the world, doesn't exist. It's just a trick that I'm pulling. It's a trick that you agree to let me pull even as I give the trick away. Somehow the trick keeps working even after you see it as a trick.

Samantha approaches the hole in the aluminum siding, the hole that is shaped like the house they fortified, and removes her off-white silk blouse. She unsnaps her nursing bra and maneuvers herself so that her left breast is filling the hole.

See what I mean?

But despite images like this one, a partially erect nipple on a breast protruding out from the wall of an industrial shed, a breast exposed to the frigid darkness outside, the illusion needed to maintain this world is mostly spoiled now. All you've really got are sentences, then words, and then letters. All that is here, all there has ever been, is my grappling with language and the paper pages where the ink has dried, but now there isn't even that, or not for very much longer.

This is my happy ending for you, and it's my confession as well. There is no story. There is no world but just a few words.

You are free to go.

ABOUT THE AUTHOR

Douglas Lain is the author of *The Fall into Time, Last Week's Apocalypse, Pick Your Battle: Your Guide to Urban Foraging, Hollywood Films, Late Capitalism, and the Communist Alternative: A Memoir*, and *Billy Moon 1968*, which is forthcoming from Tor. His work has appeared in *Amazing Stories, Strange Horizons, Lady Churchill's Rosebud Wristlet, Interzone, Polyphony 1, Pif Magazine, Flurb, The Magazine of Bizarro Fiction*, and many other publications. His stories have been chosen for inclusion in Rich Horton's Best Science Fiction of the Year 2005 and The Best of Lady Churchill's Rosebud Wristlet. Douglas Lain also hosts the Diet Soap podcast.

Visit him online at www.douglaslain.com.

Bizarro books

CATALOG   SPRING 2011

Bizarro Books publishes under the following imprints:

www.rawdogscreamingpress.com

www.eraserheadpress.com

www.afterbirthbooks.com

www.swallowdownpress.com

For all your Bizarro needs visit:

WWW.BIZARROCENTRAL.COM

Introduce yourselves to the bizarro fiction genre and all of its authors with the Bizarro Starter Kit series. Each volume features short novels and short stories by ten of the leading bizarro authors, designed to give you a perfect sampling of the genre for only $10.

BB-0X1
"The Bizarro Starter Kit"
(Orange)
Featuring D. Harlan Wilson, Carlton Mellick III, Jeremy Robert Johnson, Kevin L Donihe, Gina Ranalli, Andre Duza, Vincent W. Sakowski, Steve Beard, John Edward Lawson, and Bruce Taylor. **236 pages $10**

BB-0X2
"The Bizarro Starter Kit"
(Blue)
Featuring Ray Fracalossy, Jeremy C. Shipp, Jordan Krall, Mykle Hansen, Andersen Prunty, Eckhard Gerdes, Bradley Sands, Steve Aylett, Christian TeBordo, and Tony Rauch. **244 pages $10**

BB-0X2
"The Bizarro Starter Kit"
(Purple)
Featuring Russell Edson, Athena Villaverde, David Agranoff, Matthew Revert, Andrew Goldfarb, Jeff Burk, Garrett Cook, Kris Saknussemm, Cody Goodfellow, and Cameron Pierce **264 pages $10**

BB-001 "The Kafka Effekt" D. Harlan Wilson - A collection of forty-four irreal short stories loosely written in the vein of Franz Kafka, with more than a pinch of William S. Burroughs sprinkled on top. **211 pages $14**

BB-002 "Satan Burger" Carlton Mellick III - The cult novel that put Carlton Mellick III on the map ... Six punks get jobs at a fast food restaurant owned by the devil in a city violently overpopulated by surreal alien cultures. **236 pages $14**

BB-003 "Some Things Are Better Left Unplugged" Vincent Sakwoski - Join The Man and his Nemesis, the obese tabby, for a nightmare roller coaster ride into this postmodern fantasy. **152 pages $10**

BB-004 "Shall We Gather At the Garden?" Kevin L Donihe - Donihe's Debut novel. Midgets take over the world, The Church of Lionel Richie vs. The Church of the Byrds, plant porn and more! **244 pages $14**

BB-005 "Razor Wire Pubic Hair" Carlton Mellick III - A genderless humandildo is purchased by a razor dominatrix and brought into her nightmarish world of bizarre sex and mutilation. **176 pages $11**

BB-006 "Stranger on the Loose" D. Harlan Wilson - The fiction of Wilson's 2nd collection is planted in the soil of normalcy, but what grows out of that soil is a dark, witty, otherworldly jungle... **228 pages $14**

BB-007 "The Baby Jesus Butt Plug" Carlton Mellick III - Using clones of the Baby Jesus for anal sex will be the hip sex fetish of the future. **92 pages $10**

BB-008 "Fishyfleshed" Carlton Mellick III - The world of the past is an illogical flatland lacking in dimension and color, a sick-scape of crispy squid people wandering the desert for no apparent reason. **260 pages $14**

BB-009 "Dead Bitch Army" Andre Duza - Step into a world filled with racist teenagers, cannibals, 100 warped Uncle Sams, automobiles with razor-sharp teeth, living graffiti, and a pissed-off zombie bitch out for revenge. **344 pages $16**

BB-010 "The Menstruating Mall" Carlton Mellick III - "The Breakfast Club meets Chopping Mall as directed by David Lynch." - Brian Keene **212 pages $12**

BB-011 "Angel Dust Apocalypse" Jeremy Robert Johnson - Meth-heads, man-made monsters, and murderous Neo-Nazis. "Seriously amazing short stories..." - Chuck Palahniuk, author of Fight Club **184 pages $11**

BB-012 "Ocean of Lard" Kevin L Donihe / Carlton Mellick III - A parody of those old Choose Your Own Adventure kid's books about some very odd pirates sailing on a sea made of animal fat. **176 pages $12**

BB-015 "Foop!" Chris Genoa - Strange happenings are going on at Dactyl, Inc, the world's first and only time travel tourism company. "A surreal pie in the face!" - Christopher Moore **300 pages $14**

BB-020 "Punk Land" Carlton Mellick III - In the punk version of Heaven, the anarchist utopia is threatened by corporate fascism and only Goblin, Mortician's sperm, and a blue-mohawked female assassin named Shark Girl can stop them. **284 pages $15**

BB-021 "Pseudo-City" D. Harlan Wilson - Pseudo-City exposes what waits in the bathroom stall, under the manhole cover and in the corporate boardroom, all in a way that can only be described as mind-bogglingly irreal. **220 pages $16**

BB-023 "Sex and Death In Television Town" Carlton Mellick III - In the old west, a gang of hermaphrodite gunslingers take refuge from a demon plague in Telos: a town where its citizens have televisions instead of heads. **184 pages $12**

BB-027 "Siren Promised" Jeremy Robert Johnson & Alan M Clark
- Nominated for the Bram Stoker Award. A potent mix of bad drugs, bad dreams, brutal bad guys, and surreal/incredible art by Alan M. Clark. **190 pages $13**

BB-030 "Grape City" Kevin L. Donihe - More Donihe-style comedic bizarro about a demon named Charles who is forced to work a minimum wage job on Earth after Hell goes out of business. **108 pages $10**

BB-031 "Sea of the Patchwork Cats" Carlton Mellick III - A quiet dreamlike tale set in the ashes of the human race. For Mellick enthusiasts who also adore The Twilight Zone. **112 pages $10**

BB-032 "Extinction Journals" Jeremy Robert Johnson - An uncanny voyage across a newly nuclear America where one man must confront the problems associated with loneliness, insane dieties, radiation, love, and an ever-evolving cockroach suit with a mind of its own. **104 pages $10**

BB-034 "The Greatest Fucking Moment in Sports" Kevin L. Donihe
- In the tradition of the surreal anti-sitcom Get A Life comes a tale of triumph and agape love from the master of comedic bizarro. **108 pages $10**

BB-035 "The Troublesome Amputee" John Edward Lawson - Disturbing verse from a man who truly believes nothing is sacred and intends to prove it. **104 pages $9**

BB-037 "The Haunted Vagina" Carlton Mellick III - It's difficult to love a woman whose vagina is a gateway to the world of the dead. **132 pages $10**

BB-042 "Teeth and Tongue Landscape" Carlton Mellick III - On a planet made out of meat, a socially-obsessive monophobic man tries to find his place amongst the strange creatures and communities that he comes across. **110 pages $10**

BB-043 "War Slut" Carlton Mellick III - Part "1984," part "Waiting for Godot," and part action horror video game adaptation of John Carpenter's "The Thing." **116 pages $10**

BB-045 "Dr. Identity" D. Harlan Wilson - Follow the Dystopian Duo on a killing spree of epic proportions through the irreal postcapitalist city of Bliptown where time ticks sideways, artificial Bug-Eyed Monsters punish citizens for consumer-capitalist lethargy, and ultraviolence is as essential as a daily multivitamin. **208 pages $15**

BB-047 "Sausagey Santa" Carlton Mellick III - A bizarro Christmas tale featuring Santa as a piratey mutant with a body made of sausages. 124 pages $10

BB-048 "Misadventures in a Thumbnail Universe" Vincent Sakowski - Dive deep into the surreal and satirical realms of neo-classical Blender Fiction, filled with television shoes and flesh-filled skies. **120 pages $10**

BB-049 "Vacation" Jeremy C. Shipp - Blueblood Bernard Johnson leaved his boring life behind to go on The Vacation, a year-long corporate sponsored odyssey. But instead of seeing the world, Bernard is captured by terrorists, becomes a key figure in secret drug wars, and, worse, doesn't once miss his secure American Dream. **160 pages $14**

BB-053 "Ballad of a Slow Poisoner" Andrew Goldfarb Millford Mutterwurst sat down on a Tuesday to take his afternoon tea, and made the unpleasant discovery that his elbows were becoming flatter. **128 pages $10**

BB-055 "Help! A Bear is Eating Me" Mykle Hansen - The bizarro, heartwarming, magical tale of poor planning, hubris and severe blood loss... **150 pages $11**

BB-056 "Piecemeal June" Jordan Krall - A man falls in love with a living sex doll, but with love comes danger when her creator comes after her with crab-squid assassins. **90 pages $9**

BB-058 "The Overwhelming Urge" Andersen Prunty - A collection of bizarro tales by Andersen Prunty. **150 pages $11**

BB-059 "Adolf in Wonderland" Carlton Mellick III - A dreamlike adventure that takes a young descendant of Adolf Hitler's design and sends him down the rabbit hole into a world of imperfection and disorder. **180 pages $11**

BB-061 "Ultra Fuckers" Carlton Mellick III - Absurdist suburban horror about a couple who enter an upper middle class gated community but can't find their way out. **108 pages $9**

BB-062 "House of Houses" Kevin L. Donihe - An odd man wants to marry his house. Unfortunately, all of the houses in the world collapse at the same time in the Great House Holocaust. Now he must travel to House Heaven to find his departed fiancee. **172 pages $11**

BB-064 "Squid Pulp Blues" Jordan Krall - In these three bizarro-noir novellas, the reader is thrown into a world of murderers, drugs made from squid parts, deformed gun-toting veterans, and a mischievous apocalyptic donkey. **204 pages $12**

BB-065 "Jack and Mr. Grin" Andersen Prunty - "When Mr. Grin calls you can hear a smile in his voice. Not a warm and friendly smile, but the kind that seizes your spine in fear. You don't need to pay your phone bill to hear it. That smile is in every line of Prunty's prose." - Tom Bradley. **208 pages $12**

BB-066 "Cybernetrix" Carlton Mellick III - What would you do if your normal everyday world was slowly mutating into the video game world from Tron? **212 pages $12**

BB-072 "Zerostrata" Andersen Prunty - Hansel Nothing lives in a tree house, suffers from memory loss, has a very eccentric family, and falls in love with a woman who runs naked through the woods every night. **144 pages $11**

BB-073 "The Egg Man" Carlton Mellick III - It is a world where humans reproduce like insects. Children are the property of corporations, and having an enormous ten-foot brain implanted into your skull is a grotesque sexual fetish. Mellick's industrial urban dystopia is one of his darkest and grittiest to date. **184 pages $11**

BB-074 "Shark Hunting in Paradise Garden" Cameron Pierce - A group of strange humanoid religious fanatics travel back in time to the Garden of Eden to discover it is invested with hundreds of giant flying maneating sharks. **150 pages $10**

BB-075 "Apeshit" Carlton Mellick III - Friday the 13th meets Visitor Q. Six hipster teens go to a cabin in the woods inhabited by a deformed killer. An incredibly fucked-up parody of B-horror movies with a bizarro slant. **192 pages $12**

BB-076 "Fuckers of Everything on the Crazy Shitting Planet of the Vomit At smosphere" Mykle Hansen - Three bizarro satires. Monster Cocks, Journey to the Center of Agnes Cuddlebottom, and Crazy Shitting Planet. **228 pages $12**

BB-077 "The Kissing Bug" Daniel Scott Buck - In the tradition of Roald Dahl, Tim Burton, and Edward Gorey, comes this bizarro anti-war children's story about a bohemian conenose kissing bug who falls in love with a human woman. **116 pages $10**

BB-078 "MachoPoni" Lotus Rose - It's My Little Pony... *Bizarro* style! A long time ago Poniworld was split in two. On one side of the Jagged Line is the Pastel Kingdom, a magical land of music, parties, and positivity. On the other side of the Jagged Line is Dark Kingdom inhabited by an army of undead ponies. **148 pages $11**

BB-079 "The Faggiest Vampire" Carlton Mellick III - A Roald Dahlesque children's story about two faggy vampires who partake in a mustache competition to find out which one is truly the faggiest. **104 pages $10**

BB-080 "Sky Tongues" Gina Ranalli - The autobiography of Sky Tongues, the biracial hermaphrodite actress with tongues for fingers. Follow her strange life story as she rises from freak to fame. **204 pages $12**

BB-081 "**Washer Mouth**" **Kevin L. Donihe** - A washing machine becomes human and pursues his dream of meeting his favorite soap opera star. **244 pages $11**

BB-082 "**Shatnerquake**" **Jeff Burk** - All of the characters ever played by William Shatner are suddenly sucked into our world. Their mission: hunt down and destroy the real William Shatner. **100 pages $10**

BB-083 "**The Cannibals of Candyland**" **Carlton Mellick III** - There exists a race of cannibals that are made of candy. They live in an underground world made out of candy. One man has dedicated his life to killing them all. **170 pages $11**

BB-084 "**Slub Glub in the Weird World of the Weeping Willows**" **Andrew Goldfarb** - The charming tale of a blue glob named Slub Glub who helps the weeping willows whose tears are flooding the earth. There are also hyenas, ghosts, and a voodoo priest **100 pages $10**

BB-085 "**Super Fetus**" **Adam Pepper** - Try to abort this fetus and he'll kick your ass! **104 pages $10**

BB-086 "**Fistful of Feet**" **Jordan Krall** - A bizarro tribute to spaghetti westerns, featuring Cthulhu-worshipping Indians, a woman with four feet, a crazed gunman who is obsessed with sucking on candy, Syphilis-ridden mutants, sexually transmitted tattoos, and a house devoted to the freakiest fetishes. **228 pages $12**

BB-087 "**Ass Goblins of Auschwitz**" **Cameron Pierce** - It's Monty Python meets Nazi exploitation in a surreal nightmare as can only be imagined by Bizarro author Cameron Pierce. **104 pages $10**

BB-088 "**Silent Weapons for Quiet Wars**" **Cody Goodfellow** - "This is high-end psychological surrealist horror meets bottom-feeding low-life crime in a techno-thrilling science fiction world full of Lovecraft and magic..." -John Skipp **212 pages $12**

BB-089 "Warrior Wolf Women of the Wasteland" Carlton Mellick III
Road Warrior Werewolves versus McDonaldland Mutants...post-apocalyptic fiction has never been quite like this. **316 pages $13**

BB-090 "Cursed" Jeremy C Shipp - The story of a group of characters who believe they are cursed and attempt to figure out who cursed them and why. A tale of stylish absurdism and suspenseful horror. **218 pages $15**

BB-091 "Super Giant Monster Time" Jeff Burk - A tribute to choose your own adventures and Godzilla movies. Will you escape the giant monsters that are rampaging the fuck out of your city and shit? Or will you join the mob of alien-controlled punk rockers causing chaos in the streets? What happens next depends on you. **188 pages $12**

BB-092 "Perfect Union" Cody Goodfellow - "Cronenberg's THE FLY on a grand scale: human/insect gene-spliced body horror, where the human hive politics are as shocking as the gore." -John Skipp. **272 pages $13**

BB-093 "Sunset with a Beard" Carlton Mellick III - 14 stories of surreal science fiction. **200 pages $12**

BB-094 "My Fake War" Andersen Prunty - The absurd tale of an unlikely soldier forced to fight a war that, quite possibly, does not exist. It's Rambo meets Waiting for Godot in this subversive satire of American values and the scope of the human imagination. **128 pages $11**

BB-095 "Lost in Cat Brain Land" Cameron Pierce - Sad stories from a surreal world. A fascist mustache, the ghost of Franz Kafka, a desert inside a dead cat. Primordial entities mourn the death of their child. The desperate serve tea to mysterious creatures. A hopeless romantic falls in love with a pterodactyl. And much more. **152 pages $11**

BB-096 "The Kobold Wizard's Dildo of Enlightenment +2" Carlton Mellick III - A Dungeons and Dragons parody about a group of people who learn they are only made up characters in an AD&D campaign and must find a way to resist their nerdy teenaged players and retarded dungeon master in order to survive. **232 pages $12**

BB-097 "My Heart Said No, but the Camera Crew Said Yes!" Bradley Sands - A collection of short stories that are crammed with the delightfully odd and the scurrilously silly. **140 pages $13**

BB-098 "A Hundred Horrible Sorrows of Ogner Stump" Andrew Goldfarb - Goldfarb's acclaimed comic series. A magical and weird journey into the horrors of everyday life. **164 pages $11**

BB-099 "Pickled Apocalypse of Pancake Island" Cameron Pierce A demented fairy tale about a pickle, a pancake, and the apocalypse. **102 pages $8**

BB-100 "Slag Attack" Andersen Prunty - Slag Attack features four visceral, noir stories about the living, crawling apocalypse. A slag is what survivors are calling the slug-like maggots raining from the sky, burrowing inside people, and hollowing out their flesh and their sanity. **148 pages $11**

BB-101 "Slaughterhouse High" Robert Devereaux - A place where schools are built with secret passageways, rebellious teens get zippers installed in their mouths and genitals, and once a year, on that special night, one couple is slaughtered and the bits of their bodies are kept as souvenirs. **304 pages $13**

BB-102 "The Emerald Burrito of Oz" John Skipp & Marc Levinthal OZ IS REAL! Magic is real! The gate is really in Kansas! And America is finally allowing Earth tourists to visit this weird-ass, mysterious land. But when Gene of Los Angeles heads off for summer vacation in the Emerald City, little does he know that a war is brewing...a war that could destroy both worlds. **280 pages $13**

BB-103 "The Vegan Revolution... with Zombies" David Agranoff When there's no more meat in hell, the vegans will walk the earth. **160 pages $11**

BB-104 "The Flappy Parts" Kevin L Donihe - Poems about bunnies, LSD, and police abuse. You know, things that matter. **132 pages $11**

BB-105 "Sorry I Ruined Your Orgy" Bradley Sands - Bizarro humorist Bradley Sands returns with one of the strangest, most hilarious collections of the year. **130 pages $11**

BB-106 "Mr. Magic Realism" Bruce Taylor - Like Golden Age science fiction comics written by Freud, *Mr. Magic Realism* is a strange, insightful adventure that spans the furthest reaches of the galaxy, exploring the hidden caverns in the hearts and minds of men, women, aliens, and biomechanical cats. **152 pages $11**

BB-107 "Zombies and Shit" Carlton Mellick III - "Battle Royale" meets "Return of the Living Dead." Mellick's bizarro tribute to the zombie genre. **308 pages $13**

BB-108 "The Cannibal's Guide to Ethical Living" Mykle Hansen - Over a five star French meal of fine wine, organic vegetables and human flesh, a lunatic delivers a witty, chilling, disturbingly sane argument in favor of eating the rich.. **184 pages $11**

BB-109 "Starfish Girl" Athena Villaverde - In a post-apocalyptic underwater dome society, a girl with a starfish growing from her head and an assassin with sea anemone hair are on the run from a gang of mutant fish men. **160 pages $11**

BB-110 "Lick Your Neighbor" Chris Genoa - Mutant ninjas, a talking whale, kung fu masters, maniacal pilgrims, and an alcoholic clown populate Chris Genoa's surreal, darkly comical and unnerving reimagining of the first Thanksgiving. **303 pages $13**

BB-111 "Night of the Assholes" Kevin L. Donihe - A plague of assholes is infecting the countryside. Normal everyday people are transforming into jerks, snobs, dicks, and douchebags. And they all have only one purpose: to make your life a living hell.. **192 pages $11**

BB-112 "Jimmy Plush, Teddy Bear Detective" Garrett Cook - Hardboiled cases of a private detective trapped within a teddy bear body. **180 pages $11**